MW01168536

Destiny

A Novel of Napoleon & Josephine

Destiny

A Novel of Napoleon & Josephine

BERTRAM FIELDS

Marmont Lane
Books

MARMONT LANE
BOOKS

DESTINY: A NOVEL OF NAPOLEON & JOSEPHINE

For information address Marmont Lane Books
139 South Beverly Drive Suite 214
Beverly Hills, CA USA 90210

www.marmontlane.com

FIRST EDITION

Publisher: Bobby Woods/Marmont Lane Books

Design: ♡×☕=⚡

Engravings: Paul Rogers

ISBN 13: 978-0-9905602-0-3
ISBN 10: 990560201

Also by Bertram Fields

Royal Blood: Richard III and the Mystery of the Princes

Players: The Mysterious Identity of William Shakespeare

As D. Kincaid

The Sunset Bomber

The Lawyer's Tale

To my friend Mario Puzo,

whose play inspired this book

and who left us much too soon.

Destiny

A NOVEL OF NAPOLEON & JOSEPHINE

BERTRAM FIELDS

MARMONT LANE
BOOKS

Chapter One

THE PALE AUTUMN SUN broke through the morning mist as the tumbril clattered across the still wet cobblestones carrying twenty souls inexorably toward Dr. Guillotine's efficient device to end their lives.

Selected somewhat arbitrarily by the Committee of Public Safety, they had been called from their cells in Les Carmes Prison while Paris was still dark. Others would follow later in the day, and still others the next morning.

And so it continued day after day, the march of death. Its victims were not merely former aristocrats, as in the past, but ardent republicans, even former revolutionary leaders. France was in the grip of "the terror." The Revolution was eating itself.

One by one, the occupants of the tumbril passed through the early morning crowd of gaping citizens, mounted the stairs to the platform, lay on the rack with their necks in the aperture scientifically designed for that purpose and, praying, trembling or both, heard the whoosh of the great blade descending – the last sound they ever heard as their severed heads dropped into the waiting basket.

Across Paris, Rose de Beauharnais awakened, stretched her slender body, threw on a white silk robe and stepped to the window of her apartment. Below her, Paris was coming to life. Carriages clattered over the ancient cobblestones, working men hurried to their jobs, while women walked from the boulangerie, loaves of bread under their arms, looking upward to avoid the contents of chamber pots cavalierly thrown from Parisian windows.

Although it was a Sunday, it was still a work day. The revolutionary government had put an end to the seven day week, replacing it with a week of ten days, with only one day of rest on the tenth day. This was the same government that changed the names of all the months to things like Brumaire, Fructador and Vendémiaire and replaced the churches with "temples of reason."

Rose faced the morning with a mixture of concern and contentment, concern over her mounting debts and contentment that, unlike so many of her friends, she was still alive. Separated from her husband, she had received word the preceding week that he had been imprisoned by the Committee of Public Safety. She felt only slight remorse about Beauharnais. Their marriage had never been a good one. She did feel concern for her children, Eugene and Hortense. But they were levelheaded young adults. They would survive their father's imprisonment and even his death, should it come to that.

Rose smiled at the thought of her children. She brewed a pot of tea and considered what she should wear that day to a reception given by her new friend Theresia Tallien. As she stirred a third spoonful of sugar in the tea, she was startled by a loud pounding at the door. Who . . .?

Tightening the belt of her robe, Rose started toward the door. The pounding grew louder, and now there were shouts "Open at once in the name of the Committee of Public Safety."

Now Rose felt a cold stab of fear. "The terror" had taken her husband and many of her friends. It could take her as well.

Opening the door, she saw three large men in dirty uniforms, tri-color cockades in their hats. Their leader stepped close to Rose, his breath reeking of garlic. "Citizeness Rose de Beauharnais. You are under arrest by order of the Committee of Public Safety. You will dress and come with us at once!"

Half an hour later Rose was led by her captors into a huge fortress-like building of gray stone – the fearful Les Carmes Prison. As she entered the building, the smells and sounds were overwhelming. She winced at the odors of sweat, excrement, urine and vomit and the insane screams of a prisoner in some distant cell.

As she passed down the corridor, Rose saw women and men together in cells, many in soiled and tattered finery. A familiar looking woman in a stained velvet cape smiled warmly at Rose. She smiled back as best she could.

Now her guard opened a cell door, "Your palace, madame," he said mockingly, shoving her roughly inside.

What Rose saw in the cell shocked her, and Rose was not easily shocked. The cell contained two cots, one of which was empty. The other was occupied by a man and woman in the throes of ardent lovemaking.

At first, Rose sat on the other cot and tried to look away. But the man's grunts and the woman's moans were distracting; they seemed not to care about privacy. She watched as the couple, drenched in sweat, came to what seemed a shuddering and simultaneous climax.

After a moment, the man rose. Nodding politely to Rose, he said "Excuse me madame," as he began to put on his clothes, which had been folded neatly at the end of Rose's cot.

That evening, after Rose's cell-mate had introduced herself as Valerie du Bois, the two women found that they had friends in common. Finally, Rose found the courage to ask about Valerie's lover and whether this kind of sexual abandon was prevalent in the prison.

"Absolutely. None of us has long to live. Each day they take twenty to forty souls to the guillotine. One never knows who'll be called on any given day. Men and women frequently share a cell, and usually one can move freely from cell to cell. So the men – and many of the women too – want to squeeze as much pleasure as possible out of their last days on earth."

"And, of course, for the women there's still another motive. They want to get pregnant."

"Pregnant? With only days or weeks to live?"

"Certainly. Pregnant women are released until their child is born. Then, they must return. But at least they gain nine months of freedom, and there is always the chance of escape to the countryside and then to the border."

"For me," Valerie smiled, "both reasons apply. Besides, I'm very fond of Julian."

During the next two weeks, Rose got word that her husband had gone to the guillotine. Although their relationship had never been successful, she was surprisingly moved. A chapter in her life had ended, and, shortly, her life would end as well.

One other thing happened. One afternoon, Valerie returned from Julian's cell to tell Rose that Julian's cell-mate, Lazare Hoche, had seen Rose and found her very attractive. Hoche had suggested that they switch cells so that Julian and Valerie could be together. "And, you'll like Hoche, Rose. He's quite dashing and very amusing. Besides, I would consider it a great personal favor."

Falling into the moral code of prison life for the doomed, Rose agreed. The following night, rather shyly, she entered the cell of Lazare Hoche. Tall and powerfully built, with wavy brown hair framing a broad, handsome face, Hoche wore the faded uniform of an officer of the Revolutionary Guard. He was an educated man and had been a distinguished member of the revolutionary convention before he became a victim of "the terror."

"So, Rose, we will live together for a time – probably not long enough for us to tire of each other – I suppose that's a relief."

The man's charm and personal magnetism relaxed Rose. She smiled and curtsied.

Hoche bowed in return, and, reaching under the ragged blanket on his couch, he produced a silver flask. He unscrewed the cap and handed it to Rose. "Calvados! The best! I saved it for just such an occasion. It may be our last."

Rose raised the flask to her lips and felt the fiery liquor burn in her throat. Then, almost immediately, it created a warm and relaxed feeling in her stomach. She drank more as they passed the flask back and forth between them.

Within fifteen minutes Rose was in his arms, kissing him with a fierce passion borne of fear, Calvados and the thought that this might be her last night of lovemaking.

Soon, they were both nude and pleasuring each other in as many ways as either could devise.

Chapter Two

Napoleon Buonapart. He sounded the old name and smiled. How he had suffered French school boy jokes at his Corsican name and Italian accent.

Ah! But not now! Now he was General Napoleon Bonaparte, the hero of Toulon. At the French military academy, he had studied artillery, studied it diligently and with keen interest. He had a brain, and he had used it.

Once France had overthrown its monarchy and had adopted what was announced as a republican form of government, all of Europe mobilized to destroy those dangerous, radical ideas. Soon France was attacked from all sides, and the attacks grew more ferocious in intensity when the French government executed Louis XVI and his family.

Arrayed against the European allies was a new kind of army, the French Army of the Republic. In the other European armies, officers' commissions had to be purchased and the leadership positions were held only by aristocrats and the very wealthy, without the necessity of demonstrating any particular ability. By contrast, after a period of uncertainty and experimentation, promotion in the French army was now based essentially on merit. Brave and skilled sergeants were made officers. At first, the armies were led by a few surviving aristocratic generals like Alexandre de Beauharnais. But, as they were guillotined or took refuge outside of France, they were replaced by some men with no military background at all but, more and more, by others who had risen through the ranks based on their ability. Napoleon Bonaparte was one of these. He had military skill and was, at the same time, a staunch and outspoken republican.

Not only was most of Europe arrayed against the Republic, a revolution to restore the Bourbon monarchy had broken out in the west of France, in the Vendee, and a powerful insurgency seeking local control had arisen in Marseille and Toulon.

Toulon was under siege by the Republican forces, and the desperate citizens had turned to the British to provide food. The British fleet controlled the harbor, the largest in France. None of the French officers were able to break the siege; but a Corsican official knowing of young Captain Bonaparte recommended him to the officials in command of the siege.

Using his knowledge of artillery and its uses, Bonaparte skillfully placed his guns where they could command the harbor and began lobbing shells into the British fleet at anchor there. The British, realizing that they could be destroyed like sitting ducks, were forced to withdraw. Now with Toulon's food source gone, Bonaparte launched infantry attacks that soon took the city. He had fought in the battle himself, taking a bayonet thrust in his thigh.

Major Bonaparte's skilled and courageous conduct at Toulon had been observed by Paul Barras, the Republican government's key representative in the region. Bonaparte had made Barras look good to the government in Paris, and Barras was grateful and lavish with his praise. Bonaparte was promoted to Brigadier General.

And Barras was the man to know – a man on the rise in political circles that counted. Following Toulon, Barras and his colleagues employed a series of brilliant political maneuvers to oust Maximillien Robespierre from power. Robespierre who had been the architect of the terror, who had condemned tens of thousands to death, was sent to the guillotine himself.

The terror was over. Barras and his clique were now in charge of the government. Bonaparte was looked on by that new government as a young officer of great promise whose military skill they might very well need.

Now, General Bonaparte viewed himself in the full length mirror, adjusted his sword and prepared to ride to the office of the military high command to discuss his new assignment.

At this point, his aide entered, bowing deferentially.

"General, I know you're about to leave, but there's a young gentleman at the door. He says he must see you on an urgent matter that will take, at most, a few minutes of your time."

The aide removed the visitor's card from a small silver tray and handed it to Bonaparte. The card said simply "Eugene de Beauharnais." Glancing at the clock, Bonaparte said he would see the man – but briefly.

The aide returned with a handsome young man in an officer's uniform. The visitor bowed politely. Bonaparte remained erect.

"What is your business sir? I am pressed for time."

"A mission of mercy, General – one requiring great expediency."

"So? What is this urgent matter?"

"My mother, General, Rose de Beauharnais is imprisoned in Les Carmes. She may not have long to live. My father has already been guillotined."

"Young man, surely you know the terror is over. Many thousands have died, but, happily, no longer. General Hoche was released just yesterday to command the army in the west. I'm sure your mother will be released soon. Besides, France is hardly a safe place these days. There may be more fighting. Your mother may be safer in Les Carmes than in the streets of Paris."

"Certainly General. But my mother is quite delicate. She is from Martinique, where her family owned plantations. She will not last much longer in the damp cells at Les Carmes"

Bonaparte shrugged. "What do I care about 'plantations.' The prisons are full of rich people. I daresay richer than your mother."

As Bonaparte turned to leave, the young man gently placed his hand on the general's arm as if to stay him.

"General, before you leave, may I just show you her picture?"

Without waiting, the young man produced a miniature and handed it to Bonaparte as if it were the relic of a saint.

Bonaparte looked at the portrait of a French Mona Lisa – beautiful and seductive. He saw radiant blue eyes, glossy chestnut hair that fell in lush curls and a strange and enigmatic smile.

Somehow he felt that there was something important for him in this portrait – something he couldn't fathom. It was not just that she was alluring. It was . . . he didn't know what it was. He turned to the young man.

"Well, Beauharnais, why do you think I can help? I'm only an officer in the army of the Republic, not a politician."

"Oh no, sir, you are far more than that. You are the hero of Toulon and the protégé of Paul Barras. You've been anointed by the public as a saint of the revolution. They cannot cross you in any public matter. And this is such a small thing – just one prisoner out of thousands."

Suddenly, the young man fell to his knees. "Please General, I beg you."

"Well, let me consider the matter. My aide will let you know as soon as I have reached a decision."

Bonaparte had dinner that evening with his friend Joachim Murat, a giant cavalry officer, who knew his way around the less respectable parts of Paris.

"So, Joachim, my problem is to secure the release of this beauty from Les Carmes."

"Easy, Bonaparte. You simply ask Paul Barras. For you, he will write an order of release in ten minutes."

"No, Joachim. If I ask a favor of Barras, it will be to command the army of Italy, not to free some woman from prison."

Murat took a long drink of his wine. "Well then, you must use Bussiere."

"Bussiere?"

"Yes. He works in Les Carmes. Since the terror ended, he has a thriving business freeing prisoners who have no record of any crime."

"Well I have no idea what record this woman might have."

"It doesn't matter. Bussiere steals the records. In the winter he burns them. But, in the summer, a fire would be too suspicious, so he eats them."

"He eats them?"

"Yes, a page at a time. For 30,000 francs, he can take a little indigestion."

Bonaparte reached into the pocket of his breeches, pulling out some bills.

"Here, Joachim, fix it for me. This woman is worth far more than 30,000."

Chapter Three

Rose opened the door of her apartment with a sense of dread. In the months she had been away, she imagined that flooding, rats and dust had left the place virtually uninhabitable. To her surprise, everything was clean and in its place. Probably Hortense had dusted, scrubbed and put everything in order.

Rose's first thought was to bathe. Stripping off her ragged, filthy prison gown, she slipped into a scented bath, where she lay in a peaceful reverie for half an hour.

Then, shrugging into a robe she turned to the stack of mail stacked neatly on the hall table. Bills! Scores of unpaid demanding, frightening bills!

When she was facing the daily prospect of the guillotine, her financial difficulties were far from her thoughts. Now, finally safe, these fears came flooding back. How could she possibly meet these debts? She'd have to borrow; but from whom?

Ah well, she sighed, somehow it would work itself out. It always did. Meanwhile she had a party to attend. And Theresia Tallien's parties were always splendid.

A murmur went through the room as Rose entered Theresia's brilliantly decorated apartment. Rose knew she looked lovely, her Grecian style gown of white muslin clinging to her slim figure, her glossy chestnut hair strung with tiny spring flowers.

Theresia, a tall, dark strikingly attractive woman, greeted Rose and led her around the room introducing her to those guests she had not previously known.

There were two men present who particularly drew Rose's attention. One was Paul Barras, a large, dark complexioned man with the look of a jaded satyr. Barras was the head of the Directory and the most powerful man in France. His reputation was as a womanizer who gave legendary parties where unspeakable, but very exciting things took place. As they conversed, Barras moved ever closer until they were speaking with their lips no more than inches apart, his dark eyes locked on hers. Josephine employed all of her creole charms, seeking as if by instinct, to attract this physically aggressive male while keeping him from taking her right there in Theresia's salon with all of the guests as spectators.

After a few minutes, Barras pulled away. "Madame, it has been a great pleasure meeting you. I feel . . . I *know* . . . we will meet again. Unfortunately I must leave now. But you will hear from me. You may count on it."

As the evening wore on, Rose moved from one group to another enjoying the free flow of the comfortable conversation and the renewal of friendships she thought had gone forever. Toward the end of the evening, Rose was approached by a small, wiry man in a shabby uniform, with long greasy looking hair hanging down over his collar.

"Madame Beauharnais, I have been hoping to meet you. I am General Napoleon Bonaparte."

Surprised, Rose stifled a giggle. She had expected a tall, broad shouldered man in the dramatic and colorful uniforms affected by most of the officers she knew. Still, there was something arresting about the man. His blue eyes were intense, suggesting a depth of feeling and a high intelligence. His high cheekbones and chiseled jaw gave him a look of forceful determination.

"Ah, General, I hope you received my note. I can never adequately thank you for your efforts to free me from prison."

"I did receive your note, but your freedom is really due to the persuasive abilities of your son – a truly remarkable young man. Madame Beauharnais, I must take my leave now, may I call on you sometime soon?"

"Of course, General. It would be my pleasure."

Bonaparte bowed and hurried away in what seemed a strange and awkward movement.

As Rose was leaving, Theresia helped her into her wrap.

"So you met Bonaparte. Isn't he strange?"

"I suppose so, Theresia. But still, I owe the man a huge debt."

"And, like most men, I can imagine the payment he'll expect."

"Perhaps, Theresia; but I suspect General Bonaparte is different."

"Possibly, my dear; but I'll tell you who's not different – Paul Barras. You better be careful."

"What's the danger, Theresia, do you think I'll lose my virginity? It's a bit late for that."

* * * *

Two days later, a liveried servant arrived at Rose's door bearing an envelope with the seal of the Directory. Inside was a card with the engraved name Paul Barras.

"Ma cher Rose,

Will you do me the honor of joining me for lunch tomorrow at my home. Armand will await your reply, which I hope will be positive.

- Paul"

Rose hesitated. She realized what "lunch" certainly meant to a man like Barras. Still, she was in financial difficulty, and he was the most powerful man in France.

"Please tell Monsieur Barras I shall be delighted to attend."

* * * *

The lunch was superb. Roasted sweetbreads in a sherry sauce, Swiss chard vinaigrette and a puree of aubergine with just a hint of curry.

Barras insisted on filling and refilling Rose's wine glass with a splendid 1780 Bordeaux, successfully inducing in her a warm sense of relaxation.

When the table was cleared, Barras moved to a chair immediately next to Rose's. She was very conscious of his piercing eyes, his somewhat mocking smile.

"I have a proposition for you Rose."

"I'm not surprised."

"I think you will be. The fact is I want to help you."

"Help me?"

"Yes, I'm well aware of your perilous financial situation. As head of the Directory, I award the principal government contracts . . . supplies for the army, repairs for the streets and public buildings . . . things like that."

"But Paul, I am neither a manufacturer nor a builder . . ."

"Of course not, Rose, but manufacturers and builders will pay you handsomely to bring them lucrative contracts."

"I see . . . but what must I do in return?" Of course, she was well aware of what she must do.

Barras smiled. "Oh, the bargain . . . you must appear to be my mistress and my hostess. I require your beauty as well as your elegance and charm."

Now Rose smiled. "The hostess part is fine, but it's a bit early for the mistress part, don't you think?"

"You didn't listen Rose. I said 'appear' to be my mistress... Rose, can you keep a secret?"

"Of course."

"No, I mean it. If you betray my secret, very bad things would happen."

"To me?"

"I think you understand. Shall I tell you the secret then?"

Rose hesitated for only a instant. "Yes, Paul, I will not betray you."

"Well then, your duties as hostess will be to attend my parties and charm my guests. Your duties as my mistress will be solely to appear affectionate in public, nothing more . . . you see my preference is for young boys. Do we have an arrangement?"

Rose smiled again, laying her hand atop his, and looking deeply into his eyes. "Yes Paul, we do."

* * * *

Rose had heard about Barras' scandalous parties, but nothing had prepared her for her first evening as Barras' hostess and putative mistress.

Extraordinarily beautiful women, some dripping with diamonds, most with diaphanous gowns that revealed their breasts, moved languidly around the dramatically decorated room giving undisguised looks of lust at the somewhat older, but distinguished and handsomely tailored men.

Champagne flowed from an ice sculpture in the center of the room and liveried servants filled glass after glass for the guests, many of whom were already well on their way to a drunken state.

Rose spied General Bonaparte across the room looking scruffy as before and drinking what appeared to be tea.

In the corner of the room, a gypsy orchestra played romantic music.

As the evening wore on, Theresia Tallien danced alone, slowly disrobing until she was quite nude and then whirling faster and faster until she fell into the arms of a cavalry officer. The officer, seemingly unsurprised, lifted Theresia and carried her off to one of the many bedrooms set aside for amorous couples.

Now two other couples, partially disrobed, followed Theresia and her lover form the drawing room.

At this point, Barras moved to the center of the room to make an announcement.

"My friends, I have arranged for a rare performance this evening – one which I doubt many of you have ever seen before." He clapped his hands and into the room came a stunning blonde woman in a clinging red gown. She was leading a huge black Alsatian hound.

Seating herself on a sofa, she gave a soft command in what seemed a middle European language. The dog obediently sat and faced her, raising his paws. Slowly, the woman began massaging the dog's chest, then gradually moving her hand lower and lower, until she was stroking first his belly and then his loins.

A gasp came from the guests as the dog's penis emerged, bright red and unusually long.

The woman continued stroking the dog who was now making small groaning noises.

At this point she suddenly lifted her dress above her waist and giving another command pulled the dog's face to her own loins.

As the dog licked at her, she too began to moan and thrust her hips forward to meet his tongue. Then, in a surprisingly graceful movement, the woman fell to her hands and knees on the rug, lifting her dress once more above her waist and presenting her rear to the aroused animal.

At another hoarsely whispered command, the huge black animal mounted her from the rear, grasping her waist with his forepaws.

The crowd stared in stunned silence as the dog began rapid and furious thrusts into the woman whose mouth hung open and who soon began to moan, until finally she screamed, as she and the animal appeared to climax together.

Slowly she stood, smoothed her dress and led the dog from the room.

"Wait!" cried Rose's friend, Julie Carreau, "I want . . . the dog . . . like that, . . . now!"

Barras moved to Julie, putting his arm around her waist.

"No, Julie, not tonight. The dog is quite exhausted. You'll have to be satisfied with a less exotic form of amour."

Rose, who considered herself both experienced and broad minded, stood speechless at Barras' "entertainment." Then she felt a hand on her arm. It was Bonaparte.

"Interesting, don't you think? But not really what I want for France. It's getting late. May I drive you home?"

"Perhaps. I must speak to Paul."

Having told Barras truthfully that she had a headache, Rose left the house on Bonaparte's arm.

In his carriage, she was curious.

"What did you mean by that was not what you want for France?"

"I mean to make France a more efficient nation, to restore a sense of pride and morality."

"How will you impose your views on the nation, General?"

"I'm not sure yet, but I'll find the way."

As the carriage pulled up before Rose's apartment, Bonaparte turned to her and softly asked if he could come in.

"Not tonight, General, not tonight."

"One more thing then, my beautiful new friend – I think . . . no I'm sure . . . I'm in love with you."

"We haven't said more than ten words. You must fall in love very easily."

"No I don't. In fact, I've never been in love before."

"Then, General, you are, I think . . . no I'm sure . . . a lunatic. Good night."

She kissed him on the cheek and was gone.

Chapter Four

France had become a sea of ferment. Royalists within the country were plotting to restore the Bourbon Monarchy, and the Vendée was still in open rebellion against the revolutionary government. Now, dangerous insurgent mobs, enraged at inflation, food shortages and the corrupt inefficiency of government leaders were taking to the Paris streets urged on by both radical and pro-royalist agitators.

As the mobs grew in size, strength and ferocity, the leaders of the government took shelter in the Tuilleries Palace. Their power – their very survival – hung in the balance. Most were regicides, that is, they had voted to execute Louis XVI. If Paris fell to the insurgents, they were as good as dead. And so was the revolution.

At virtually the last moment, Barras, the principal leader of the governing clique, called upon General Bonaparte. It was almost too late; but Bonaparte assured Barras that he would deal with the situation. Sizing up the disposition of the threatening forces, Bonaparte realized at once that artillery was essential. He dispatched Joachim Murat to appropriate the cannons held in a neighboring town. Riding at top speed, Murat and his men seized the cannons and quickly dragged them back to Paris. Then, Bonaparte placed his guns strategically.

A rebel force was massed on the left bank at each of three bridges across the Seine, ready to cross to the right bank to join a larger mob on that side of the river. The right bank insurgents, screaming and wielding club, knives, rifles and pitchforks, rushed toward the Tuilleries down the rue Honore, formally the rue St. Honore. There, near the steps of the church of St. Roch, they encountered a squadron of riflemen, whose initial volley stopped them momentarily. When the mob regrouped and started forward again, a sharp command was heard. The riflemen separated quickly to each side of the street, revealing a battery of cannons that had been hidden behind them and that were aimed directly at the oncoming mob.

Not fully grasping their peril, the insurgents charged. Another command was heard, and the cannons fired volley after volley of deadly grapeshot ripping row upon row of the mob to bloody shreds and littering the steps of St. Roch with torn bodies. Soon, the rest of the mob broke up and fled in utter panic.

Bonaparte had also placed cannons on the right bank entrance to each of the bridges across the Seine. The sound of cannon fire from the rue Honore was Bonaparte's signal for his cannons on the bridges to fire into the crowds massed on the other side. These guns only had to fire once or twice to send the rebels fleeing down all the streets leading away from the river. Bonaparte had broken the back of the insurgency with just a few shots from strategically placed artillery.

Now, the Directory took control of France, and Barras took control of the Directory. Bonaparte was promoted to Major General. He was now an indispensable man to the Directors and an idol to the people – at least of those who had not been in rebellion.

Chapter Five

Rose de Beauharnais was still very much in the mind of General Bonaparte. Rejection only increased the general's ardor. Yes, there were younger women present at the dinners and balls to which he was now invited – some were prettier in a conventional way; but Rose, with her feminine grace and exotic beauty outdid them all. Time after time, Bonaparte pressed Rose to dine with him alone, making it quite plain that he intended more than dinner. Time after time, Rose used the excuse of her widowhood, even though all Paris gossiped that she was having an affair with Paul Barras, whose affection she now appeared to share with her friend, Theresia Tallien.

But Bonaparte was not one to give up easily. He managed the siege of Rose as he had the siege of Toulon. He threw his heart, soul and brain into the pursuit of his goal. He pleaded, he bellowed, he wrote her love poems and daily letters pouring out his passion.

Finally, Bonaparte's unstoppable energy and ardor gradually wore her down, but other factors contributed. Bonaparte had power and influence and Rose was deeply in debt.

Soon, the two were dining together, and ultimately – after a time – they became lovers. As soon as this occurred, Bonaparte made a strange demand. Her name must no longer be Rose. That was her name in her "old life." Her new name must be Josephine – "Yes – Josephine! You must now think of yourself as Josephine!" And, from that moment, she did.

Their lovemaking was something of an educational process. Before this, Bonaparte's limited sexual experiences had been brief and perfunctory. Rose – now Josephine – showed him a whole new world. She directed him to lie on his back while her feather light touch moved from the soles of his feet up his legs and inner thighs to his groin, where the stroke of her fingernails across his scrotum had him groaning and squirming with pleasure. This heavenly torture would continue until she would take him in her mouth and bring him to the kind of climax he had never before experienced or even dreamed of.

And it was not all one sided. Josephine relished sex, and he became her willing pupil. She taught him where and how to use his mouth, his tongue, his fingers and even his toes. She told him he must do obeisance to the "three islands of Martinique" and taught him to stop and remain still when inside her, letting each feel the other pulsate before starting his movement again.

Like his sex life, General Bonaparte's career was on the rise. After putting down the mob, he was rewarded by the government he had saved. They provided him with splendid new quarters and a handsome carriage in which he drove proudly through the Parisian streets. Most importantly, he was given command of the Army of Italy, a prime military assignment. Impressed with Josephine's son Eugene, Bonaparte made the young man his aide.

But Josephine's situation was not markedly improving. She was not getting any younger, and no one other than Bonaparte was seeking her favor. Lazare Hoche, released from prison, had commanded troops in the Vendée. Later, he traveled to Paris with the vague notion of possibly divorcing his wife and marrying Josephine. But news of the birth of his child drove those thoughts from his mind. He returned to his wife, no longer to be a factor in Josephine's life.

Meanwhile, Bonaparte began to press Josephine to marry him. At first, the idea seemed ludicrous. Despite his energy, his brain and his growing power, the man was short, strange and, while his finances had improved, he was far from wealthy.

The last factor was important to Josephine, since she spent money far beyond the small allowance sent by her mother and what she had received from Beauharnais. Constantly in debt and regularly pressing friends for loans to pay off other loans, Josephine was in a financial dilemma. If she could not reign in her spending, she was doomed. And she could not.

But, out there, standing by, was Bonaparte, a man whose intellect and intensity fascinated her, a hero, who, while not yet wealthy, was now powerful enough to eliminate any threat to her well being – financial or otherwise.

So, one day, when he proposed once again, she surprised him. She said "yes."

When Theresia Tallien asked her if she loved her future husband, Josephine's reply was characteristically straightforward. "I don't love him, Theresia, but I don't want him to go away either."

Together, Bonaparte and Josephine viewed a prospective home in the country at Malmaison, five miles from Paris. The building had clean, attractive lines. The rooms were well laid out and gave the promise of being transformed into an attractive and comfortable home. And the garden! The garden, as it was, captivated Josephine. But she could visualize what it could be, given her own imagination, taste and love for growing things.

She pleaded with Bonaparte to buy it at once, on the spot.

"My sweet Josephine. I hate denying you anything. But even you can see that it's far too expensive to be acquired and maintained on a soldier's pay. Maybe someday."

"You think someday?" she asked softly.

"Of course," he said. Why not? It was just a future "maybe"; and, even if she considered it a firm promise, it was not one he'd have to keep.

Now Bonaparte faced an unpleasant task. He had to break the news of the impending marriage to his family – his four brothers and three sisters and, of course, his mother. Letizia Bonaparte was a strong and stubborn Corsican matriarch. As a young girl, she had fought as a partisan in the Corsican revolution. That fierceness still radiated from her piercing black eyes.

Bonaparte's sisters already envied and loathed Josephine, whom they felt acted like a grand lady, but, in reality, was a common tramp and the mistress of Paul Barras. Letizia inevitably referred to her as "La Putain," the whore. Bonaparte knew his news would not be well received; but the family would have to live with it, and he had to get it over with.

To make the announcement, Bonaparte gathered the entire family together at dinner, with Josephine seated proudly on his left. As they were seated, he stood, raised his glass and announced that his beloved Josephine had consented to become his wife – that it was "destiny's touch."

His sister, Pauline, raced from the room, doubled over, retching, her hand covering her mouth. His brothers Joseph and Jerome sat in stunned silence. "Destiny's touch?" muttered Letizia, under her breath, "it's the touch of the Devil."

Chapter Six

Two weeks later, on her wedding day, Josephine waited with two witnesses and a bored civil clerk in the clerk's shabby Paris office. They waited hours for the prospective groom, who was finalizing his plans for the Italian campaign and conferring with his staff. After two hours had passed, Josephine continued to sit patiently, but the clerk left, turning the job over to his assistant.

Finally, three hours after the appointed time, Bonaparte arrived. He awakened the assistant clerk, who protested that he had never before performed a marriage ceremony and wasn't sure he was duly authorized.

Grabbing him by the collar, Bonaparte pulled him to his feet "You'll damn well perform this wedding or I'll have you shot!"

The clerk shrugged and asked to see the birth certificates of the bride and groom. Bonaparte had not had time to obtain his birth certificate, so he handed over his brother's. It showed him to be twenty-eight. Josephine said her certificate was unavailable, but she said she was twenty-nine. After all, being one year older than her husband was nothing extraordinary. In fact, she was thirty-two, which probably explains why her birth certificate was "unavailable."

Anxious to be done with it, the clerk accepted Josephine's statement. Stifling a yawn, he pulled the couple before him and performed what he thought was a proper civil ceremony.

When the brief ceremony was concluded, Bonaparte took Josephine in his arms, kissing her tenderly. "I meant what I said before. This is destiny's touch. We will be together always."

CHAPTER SEVEN

TWO DAYS AFTER THEIR MARRIAGE, Bonaparte left his bride to take command of the Army of Italy.

Once he was gone, Josephine turned her attention to Malmaison, a dream she had by no means forgotten. Giving Bonaparte's "someday" a very broad interpretation – after all, two months had passed since their visit to the property – Josephine proceeded to buy the country house, making the down payment with loans arranged by Barras. How to pay off the balance, redecorate and maintain the property were problems she put off for some other time. She had the country home she had always yearned for, and she was never going to let it go.

On his arrival in Italy, Bonaparte quickly realized that the men of his command were ill-equipped, ill-disciplined and disillusioned. He immediately turned his prodigious energy and imagination to correcting the situation. Working tirelessly, he rounded up the needed equipment (including 12,000 pairs of new boots). He set about instilling discipline and esprit de corps, dazzling them with promises. He would lead them, he said, not only to historic victories, but also "into the most fertile plains in the world" where "rich provinces and great cities will lie in your power, and you will find there honor, glory and riches."

This was in accord with Bonaparte's view that an army

advancing far from its home base must be supplied at the expense of the country in which it was fighting. His men lived off any country they invaded, taking poultry, eggs, vegetables and whatever else they could carry.

The Army of Italy was facing two allied foes, the Italians and the Piedmontese. Although outnumbered by the enemy forces Bonaparte was undeterred. He had his plan, and he had unshakeable belief in his personal skill, his ability to lead men and his luck.

Through a series of lightning-like moves and forced marches, Bonaparte succeeded in splitting the Piedmontese army from the Italians and then fighting each separately. Soon the Piedmontese sued for peace, and Bonaparte turned the full fury of his assault on the Italians.

In a brief period, Bonaparte's army of Italy had changed from a disgruntled bunch of individuals to a spirited fighting unit. Now they took pride in the duration and speed of their marches. Having seen that their new general's tactics baffled and defeated the enemy generals, they rushed into battle, believing in him and in their own ability to win against any odds. In addition, he imbued them with something the Austrians could never have. As part of the army of the French Republic, they were fighting for a country that was their own, not that of pampered aristocrats. They charged into battle shouting "*Vive La Republique*!" and they meant it.

In short order, Bonaparte's reshaped Army of Italy

had won six key battles, killed thousands of the enemy and captured thousands more, along with twenty-one enemy battle flags and forty cannons. These trophies were promptly sent back to Paris, where the public talked of nothing but General Bonaparte's masterful victories.

But Bonaparte's personal life was less gratifying. At least once a day, he wrote Josephine. His letters were passionate and quite graphic in expressing his physical lust for her. They grew stronger and stronger in imploring her to join him in Italy, and in deploring the infrequency with which she responded.

But there were reasons for Josephine's reluctance to join her husband in Italy and the paucity of her letters. The new bride was in the throes of a passionate love affair.

The revolution had brought about a profound change in the social mores of the French – or at least of the Parisians. Marriage had become a temporary arrangement, easily terminated by either party at the earliest change of heart or the first encounter with someone who seemed more attractive than one's spouse.

Adultery became almost ubiquitous. Women stopped all pretense at shyness and modesty. They stared at attractive men with looks that conveyed an invitation to erotic adventure, an invitation often accepted.

This was the atmosphere in which Josephine had been living and basically enjoying. It formed her attitude toward her marriage. She had married Bonaparte for reasons that had nothing to do with love. Having gone through a perfunctory civil ceremony and having spent only two nights with her new husband before he left for the wars, if Josephine felt any marital bond at all, it was an extremely slim one. Basically, she continued to live after her marriage just as she had before.

Shortly after Bonaparte left for Italy, Josephine met Hippolyte Charles, a dashingly handsome and highly amusing young cavalry officer. With his black curls, olive skin and flashing blue eyes, Charles was a splendid figure in his sky blue uniform with its dramatic fur lined cape and tall shako hat. His unique wit could make Josephine laugh for hours on end. With little discretion, no appreciation of the delicacy of her situation and no thought whatsoever of her husband, Josephine was soon enjoying night after night in the arms of Lieutenant Charles.

She had no intention of leaving Paris, Malmaison and her new lover for life in an army encampment with a man she hardly knew and certainly didn't love.

Josephine sat with Theresia Tallien over tea, the two laughing in amusement at Bonaparte outrageously passionate letters.

"You will come won't you?" Josephine read, holding a letter before her. "You will be with me, in my heart, in my arms, on my lips."

But wait, she held up her hand "Here's the best part, 'A kiss on your heart, and then another a little lower, much lower, *much lower*'; and look – Theresia, when he underlined 'much lower,' his pen punched right through the paper."

"My God, the man is mad, or at least madly in love. You must be just a little pleased to have the idol of all Paris adore you so."

"I suppose so, Theresia. But you know my present feelings lie elsewhere."

"I do, *ma cher*, but be careful about those 'feelings.' You are the wife of a national hero. Perhaps you should be somewhat more discreet."

Bonaparte, who was always superstitious, fell into a dark mood when the glass on the miniature portrait of Josephine shattered, seemingly without cause. Turning to a fellow officer he confided "Either my wife is very ill or she is unfaithful." Of course, he feared her adultery more than her illness.

Bonaparte's letters turned now from pleading to insisting. He threatened to abandon his command and come to Josephine if she would not come to him. Ultimately, the situation came to the attention of Barras. He ordered Josephine to join her husband at once. The Directorate wanted no risk of Bonaparte leaving the command that was bringing them all glory and an enthusiastic public.

On her arrival in Milan, Josephine was installed in the massive Serbelloni Palace. She was greeted by the Duc de Serbelloni who gave her a personal tour of the rose colored palace fronted by towering Ionic columns and decorated with priceless Renaissance and baroque paintings and sculpture. The decor had been enhanced by Bonaparte who, to delight Josephine, had shipped priceless works of art to the palace from Italian cities conquered by his army.

By the time the tour was completed, Bonaparte had arrived from his headquarters. Excited as a schoolboy, he took Josephine by the hand and led her proudly to their lavishly decorated quarters with its enormous fur covered bed. He tried to keep her in that bed for as much of the next forty-eight hours as possible. When they were not in bed, they dined together and took walks in the palace gardens. When their time together was up, Bonaparte regretfully returned to his army in the field, leaving Josephine at the palace.

In Bonaparte's absence, Josephine's friends arrived from Paris to share her "exile." Gradually, Josephine became the toast of Milan, presiding at balls and receiving dignitaries from Italy and many other countries. Rich gifts poured in from those seeking to gain the favor of the wife of the now famous French General, hoping that this would gain the favor of the general himself.

Surprisingly, now that he was gone again, Josephine found that she rather missed Bonaparte. She missed his intensity and sharp intelligence. She also missed being unconditionally adored throughout the day and night.

After a time, Bonaparte sent for her to join him at his field headquarters in Brescia. When she arrived, he greeted her effusively and expressed his adoration physically, and not only in private. Subordinate officers turned away in embarrassment when their general caressed his wife passionately in public, kissing her ears and neck and even planting delicate kisses on her breasts. He remained desperately in love.

One afternoon, as Josephine and Bonaparte sipped coffee on the terrace, Josephine looked up and pointed out numerous white objects that seemed to be descending the distant mountains. Bonaparte leapt to his feet, shouting for an aide. He recognized at once that what Josephine had seen was the advance guard of the Austrian army. They had moved unobserved through the Brenner Pass and were now rapidly descending to attack Bonaparte's flank.

Without waiting to form up his men, Bonaparte rushed Josephine into a coach and sent her off toward Milan with a guard of thirty dragoons to prevent her being cut off and captured by the Austrians.

The military escort proved necessary. As they passed along the shore of Lake Guarda, an Austrian gunboat raced toward them from a position near the opposite shore. The sight was particularly frightening, since the boat was one of the recently developed vessels powered by steam. As the strange looking craft drew near, its bow gun began to fire in their direction. Bonaparte's aide pushed Josephine out of the coach and into a ditch. Josephine's dragoons dismounted and raked the gunboat with deadly rifle fire, killing its gun crew and smashing the window of its bridge. Soon the gunboat steamed away and the party was able to proceed. Obviously, however, the Austrians were here in force, and the attack made Josephine fear not only for herself but, to her surprise, for Bonaparte.

She need not have feared for him. In a series of lightning movements and all night marches, Bonaparte drove the Austrians out of Northern Italy, fighting legendary battles at Rivoli and Arcola. In an act of enormous bravery, Bonaparte led a charge across the bridge at Arcola, waiving the tri-color flag in one hand and shouting "*suive moi!*" (follow me!). Screaming and shooting, his men followed him along the bridge until murderous Austrian rifle and cannon fire drove them back. Undaunted, Bonaparte led his men along the river bank to a shallow crossing point, and then led them crashing into the Austrian's flank, overwhelming them. Bonaparte's flag waiving bravery on the bridge at Arcola was widely celebrated and was memorialized in a famous painting by Antoine-Jean Gros. He was now revered by the French as a man of enormous personal bravery, as well as a brilliant and successful general.

With the Italian campaign well in hand, Bonaparte wanted nothing more than to be once again with his adored Josephine. He wrote her each day – sometimes from his tent, sometimes during a pause in a long and arduous march. The letters were no less graphic than before in expressing his love and physical desire for her.

"How happy I would be if I could assist at your undressing, the little firm white breasts, the adorable face, the hair tied up in a scarf *a la creole*. You know that

I never forget the little visits, you know, the little black forest . . . I kiss it a thousand times in memory and wait impatiently for the moment I will be in it again. To live within Josephine is to live in the Elysian fields. Kisses on your mouth, your eyes, your breast, everywhere, *everywhere*."

But it was not to be quite yet. After laying siege to Mantua, Bonaparte moved swiftly through the Alpine passes to attack Austria from the south, with orders from the Directorate to join up with the French armies of the Rhine.

These were orders Bonaparte intended to ignore. He was not anxious to share the glory of Austria's defeat with Generals Hoche and Jourdan, who commanded the armies on the Rhine. With his usual swift movements, he soon brought his troops to within striking distance of Vienna. The Imperial Court, in a state of panic, were packing to flee, remembering that the French republicans had killed Louis XVI and his Austrian queen.

But Bonaparte had no intention of murdering the Austrian Imperial family. He was no regicide; and the time might come when he would need an Austrian alliance. He offered an armistice to the surprised Austrians and planned to negotiate peace terms before Hoche and Jourdan could arrive on the scene.

Now Bonaparte could return to Josephine. They lived together for a time in the countryside near Milan. It was a different, more assured Bonaparte. Senior officers were astonished at his quiet but commanding tone, the piercing eyes that now seemed to look right through them. Now, General Bonaparte was not only a hero, but a conqueror.

And his men worshiped him. He had fulfilled his promises. They had prospered in the rich valleys of Northern Italy just as he had said they would. Officers returned to France, bringing with them wagons loaded with Italian art, plate and jewelry. Ordinary soldiers had not only eaten well, even they had stuffed their pockets with coins and jewels. Bonaparte, himself, sent back to Paris the famed lion of Venice and the four bronze horses that had stood atop St. Mark's Cathedral. Most important of all, he had led them all – officers and men alike – to glory.

Although changed in his demeanor in dealing with men, he was unchanged in his passion for Josephine. Once again, officers and their ladies gossiped about his tendency to kiss and fondle his wife in public. And, in private, he reveled in acting out the fantasies of his letters.

It was in this period that Josephine demonstrated her extraordinary abilities as consort of a man who was already treated as near royalty. She presided graciously at luncheons, dinner and balls and provided witty conversation at small functions. She was warm and pleasant to everyone except Bonaparte's family, most of whom visited his Italian Palace in this period and remained adamant in loathing Josephine.

Together again, Bonaparte and Josephine seemed to grow closer. While she was not yet ready to admit to herself that she loved him – and while her thoughts still drifted from time to time to Hippolyte Charles – she had come to have enormous respect for Bonaparte and even to enjoy his company.

He continued to love her desperately.

Chapter Eight

Now Bonaparte turned to the peace negotiations. He found that the same arrogance and short sightedness that had characterized the Austrian military leadership characterized the Austrian negotiators as well. Accustomed to the discipline and logic of his military operations, his patience turned to rage as, day after day, he encountered what he considered the blindness and stupidity of the aristocratic Austrian diplomats.

At one session, hearing a particularly inane and bellicose response from the Austrians, he rose and shouted "Your empire is nothing more than an old hag of a servant whom everyone in the house rapes." Smashing a plate against the wall, he stormed from the hall, threatening as he left "All right – you can have your war!"

His tantrum seemed to work. The Austrians urged him to return to the bargaining table and ultimately accepted a treaty immensely favorable to France.

Now Bonaparte had become the most famous and admired man in France. The name of the street in which he lived was changed by the Paris Municipal Counsel from Rue Chatereine to Rue de la Victoire (Street of the Victory). His picture was in homes and shop windows throughout France.

As Germaine de Stael put it "He was the hope of every man, republican or royalist; all saw the present and the future as held in his strong hands."

A formal gathering to welcome the returning hero was held in the courtyard of the Luxembourg Palace. The crowd was so large, it spilled over from the courtyard to all of the adjoining streets and buildings. The five Directors were there in their colorful uniforms, as were the members of the Counsel of Five Hundred in their red togas intended to evoke thoughts of the Roman Senate. A huge orchestra stuck up a tune specially composed for Bonaparte, as he stepped forward – a small figure in his plain, unadorned uniform – but a figure now revered by a grateful nation.

Now that he was back in Paris and basking in public adulation, Bonaparte turned his attention to his next assignment. As he had learned in battle, when you strike a successful blow, follow it up, move forward, seize the victory.

But where could he strike hardest to advance his career? He received advice on the subject from a new source, an extraordinary man, who would play a critical part in Bonaparte's life. Charles-Maurice de Talleyrand-Perigord had once been the Bishop of Autun, but that religious office had not affected his lifestyle in the slightest. Good food, fine wine and seducible women occupied the part of his life that was not taken up with self-enrichment.

Highly intelligent, articulate and brutally cynical, Talleyrand had turned from the church to the arena of political intrigue. Recognizing that the excesses of the revolution placed him a serious danger, he had sensibly taken refuge for a time in the United States. Now, with the terror at an end, he had happily returned to France and resumed his political scheming. Recognizing Bonaparte as a rising star, he sought to make himself indispensable to the popular, young general.

On a rainy afternoon, Talleyrand entered Bonaparte's book-lined study. Born with a club foot, he had adopted an odd kind of gliding walk to conceal it. Sidling toward Bonaparte in this peculiar manner, he bowed as if in a royal court. The gesture was not lost on the general.

"You said, Talleyrand, that you had some advice for me."

"I do indeed, general. But first, may I help myself to some of the cognac I see there on your console?"

Talleyrand glided to the console and poured himself a glass of the golden liquor.

"*Salut*" he said raising his glass to Bonaparte. "The weather is miserable. This warms me."

"Monsieur – if you please. I'm terribly busy. What is this advice you wish to impart?"

"Egypt. That's it."

"Egypt? What do you mean?"

"Just that. You've been asking yourself a question 'What can I do now?' That's the answer."

"You don't want to command an army on the Rhine. Yes, I know there's supposedly peace with Austria.

But there will still be thankless and dangerous battles to be fought out there, with little glory to be earned and significant risk to your reputation – even your life. Besides, the armies on the Rhine are commanded by successful generals more senior than you. It would create an enormous problem if you demanded that they serve in a subordinate position; and, certainly, you would not want to serve in such a position yourself.

"Egypt is a different story entirely. No significant opposition – only primitive Mamelukes and toothless Turks, a chance to hurt the British by interfering with their Indian trade and, most important of all, it will sound quite splendid to the public. There is glory and plunder to be had without any significant risk."

"What about the Directory?"

"They will not oppose you. France has lost its colonies in North America and India. A new colony will be a welcome idea – even to politicians who constantly chant that all men are created equal and have the right to self-government."

* * * *

"Egypt?" queried a surprised Josephine that evening. "Why Egypt?"

"Because, my little rabbit, by taking Egypt I can cut off England's control of India, doing her massive damage. Besides, I will bring scientists and engineers with me who can study the antiquities of Egypt and perhaps, by taming the Nile, I can make it once again a country of immense wealth – a rich country entirely controlled by France."

He had not given her the cynical part of the explanation provided by Talleyrand. That was better kept between himself and the former Bishop.

By this time, Josephine had come to have affectionate feelings for Bonaparte, and it was only human to realize the advantages of marriage to a man cherished by an entire nation. She began to worry that Bonaparte would learn of her affair with Hippolyte Charles; and, hearing of the death of Lazare Hoche, she was terrified that her love letters to Hoche, written shortly after they were both released from prison, would be made public. At this point Charles came to her rescue. Using his formidable charms on the widow Hoche, he managed to obtain the letters and return them to a grateful Josephine who immediately burned them.

Meanwhile Bonaparte had convinced the Directory to finance his Egyptian campaign. After months of arduous preparation, he was ready to put the plan in action. On his flagship, L'Orient, Josephine said goodbye to her husband and also to her son, Eugene, who was to accompany Bonaparte as his aide, as he had during the Italian campaign. Eugene was now seventeen. He was a handsome, athletic young man of proven bravery. He possessed his mother's easygoing charm and was becoming most attractive to Parisian women.

Within months of his departure, Bonaparte's

troops had taken Malta, and he had landed his army near Alexandria, accompanied by hundreds of scientists, archeologists and engineers. The expedition already seemed a success. Soon, French engineers were planning the ways in which Egypt could be converted into a prosperous region, French archeologists were seeking to uncover the mysteries of this ancient culture and Bonaparte set in motion a plan to rule the region through Islamic religious leaders.

Egypt at the time was theoretically part of the Ottoman Empire, but it was actually ruled by the Mamelukes, a feudal tribe of ferocious horsemen. In a series of successful campaigns, Bonaparte defeated the fierce but primitive army of the Mamelukes. Their horsemen were no match for disciplined and efficient French formations.

Then, at the Battle of the Pyramids, he defeated a Turkish force, even though it was supported by a crack British unit. He had attained control of Egypt and a substantial part of the Middle East, and his army of scientists and archeologists pursued their study of all things Egyptian, creating the field now known as Egyptology.

But he had not made sufficient allowance for the British Navy and its great admiral, Horatio Nelson. Ten days after the Battle of the Pyramids, a British squadron commanded by Nelson discovered the French fleet still in the harbor of Alexandria. In a single day and night, the entire French fleet was destroyed. Only a handful of smaller ships survived.

Bonaparte realized at once that his army was cut off and would ultimately wither and die. He knew he must find as way to return to Paris while his victory at the Battle of the Pyramids still had the public's attention and before the true impact of Nelson's destruction of the fleet could be perceived. He knew the governing Directory had become extremely unpopular and that he was still considered a national hero. That status would help if he moved quickly.

As he pondered his next move, Bonaparte got more bad news – personal news that tore at his emotions like nothing before. His longtime friend, General Junot, asked to speak to him in private. Bonaparte's aides and guards were shooed from the room.

"My friend, I must tell you something that has festered in my heart for some time. Now, however, you are entitled to know. Your wife has long been involved in an affair with a young officer. She continues this affair even as we speak."

"No!" Bonaparte rose and pounded the table. "It cannot be!"

"But it is. Everyone in Paris has seen them together – even seen them embracing. They are not discreet. The man has spent many nights with your wife, and they have traveled together. I am afraid there is no doubt of this whatsoever. If there had been – if there were any chance that it was only vicious gossip – I would never have told you."

"What is the name of this man? I will have him killed!"

"He is Hippolyte Charles, an officer in the Hussars. And, Bonaparte, killing him will not undo what has occurred."

"It will damn well make me feel better!"

Bonaparte sat down again. "Junot, I must return at once to Paris. I will obtain an immediate divorce. Is there a reliable ship in the harbor that can make the voyage successfully?"

"Yes, there are one or two. And the rest of us can deal with the military situation here. Our problem is transport, not fighting an enemy."

"Arrange it Junot . . . and thank you."

At this point, Bonaparte's Sicilian sense of revenge took possession of him. Almost at once, he began an affair with the flirtatious wife of a junior officer. The affair gave him some sense of satisfaction, but not enough. His rage at Josephine continued and he recognized that the political situation also required a swift return to France.

Within weeks, Bonaparte was aboard a fast frigate accompanied by Roustum, a nineteen year old Mameluke, who had become his servant, and by Eugene Beauharnais, who loyally continued as his aide. With favorable winds and exceptional luck they hoped to make France without encountering the British navy.

CHAPTER NINE

JOSEPHINE SAT OPPOSITE HIPPOLYTE CHARLES on the terrace of their hotel in Nice. It was a difficult afternoon. After months of agonizing over the decision, she had come to the conclusion that she and Charles must part. Her life was now with her husband; and, while Charles amused and delighted her in many ways, her feelings for him had diminished over time, while her feelings for Bonaparte had increased. She had come to value his extraordinary mind, even to revel in his undiminished passion for her. He was a loving and devoted stepfather to her children, and he had brought her rank, respect and relative financial ease.

She told Charles of her decision at breakfast that morning. He had borne the news with a smile. To Charles, women were like the Paris-Orleans coach. If you missed today's coach, there would be another tomorrow. Now, they were having a farewell aperitif.

Suddenly, they heard a shout from the hotel lobby. A waiter emerged from the lobby grinning and pumping his arm in the air.

"What is it, *garçon*?" asked Charles.

"Great news, sir! General Bonaparte has returned. He is once again in France!"

Josephine paled and stood, trembling. "Oh my God! Hippolyte, I must get to Paris before he does. If he arrives at an empty house and inquires where I am . . . you can imagine."

Within an hour, Josephine was on her way. The following evening, she arrived in Lyon. Stopping only briefly to change horses, she heard devastating news, "General Bonaparte passed through here this morning. The people lined the streets cheering."

When Bonaparte arrived at their home on the rue St. Victoire, Josephine, of course, was nowhere to be found. This further enraged an already distraught Bonaparte, particularly when told she was in the South of France. He could well imagine what she was doing there and with whom she was doing it.

In a fury, he ordered her clothes packed up and deposited in the driveway. He gave instructions that she was not to be permitted in the house. Then, tortured by jealousy and rage, he went to his bedroom and tried to sleep.

Eight hours later, Josephine's carriage finally reached rue St. Victoire. With terror, she saw her trunks stacked in the driveway. She could imagine what they contained.

When she knocked at the front door, she was greeted by their aged footman, who told her with regret that the General's order had been to deny her entrance. It took time, but she finally persuaded the man to admit her. She rushed up the staircase to their bedroom and pounded on the locked door.

"Bonaparte, let me in. I can explain everything. I love you. Please let me in."

Silence.

"Please Bonaparte, I beg you let me in so that I can hold you – so that I can make you understand."

More silence.

Now the enormity of what was happening hit her. She threw herself to the floor outside the bedroom door weeping and screaming.

For an hour her sobbing continued. Then still lying on the floor, she fell into an exhausted sleep. For just a second, on the instant of her awakening, she forgot the situation. It was still dark and, at once, her plight came back to her. Still prone on the floor outside his bedroom door, her weeping and moaning began again and continued for hours softer than before, but certainly audible to Bonaparte.

Just before dawn, the bedroom door finally opened. Bonaparte stepped out. Without a word, he lifted Josephine to her feet; and, putting his arm around her waist, he led her into the bedroom. Later that morning, the staff was delighted to find the general and his wife still in bed and in each other's arms.

He had forgiven her, but a corner had been turned in their relationship. Aging, childless and now genuinely afraid of losing him, Josephine became a loving, gracious wife, attempting, in everything she did, to please him. For the rest of her life, she would never take another lover.

Bonaparte continued to adore her. But he had been badly hurt. He now saw her as she really was, not as the perfect goddess of his fervid imagination. In the long run, their relationship did not suffer from this. It gained. But there was still another change. He felt now that he could and should turn to other women, as he had at the end of his Egyptian tour. He tried not to think of this as a form of revenge – of evening the score. But he was never sure.

A week later, Bonaparte lunched with his brother Joseph at a bistro in the Marais District of Paris. Joseph was concerned.

"The news from Egypt – the total situation there is bound to come out. You will be accused of abandoning your army."

"That will be said, Joseph. But my victory at the Battle of the Pyramids – against a British unit mind you – it will overwhelm the attacks. Look at the enthusiastic welcome that greeted me in Lyon and every town on the way to Paris from the crowd. And our brother Lucien has been named President of the Council in my honor. No, the accusation of abandonment will be drowned in a sea of public adulation."

"Perhaps, but your behavior toward your wife and major Charles threatens you as well."

"What do you mean?"

"All Paris knows about your wife's affair with this man Charles. All Paris knows that their brave, bold, audacious general has forgiven his adulterous wife like a meek kitten. That will not help our cause."

"Then to hell with 'our cause'! She's my wife, and I

love her. She made a mistake. She's human. What do they want? Must I kill him?"

"That, of course, would be ideal; but it can easily be arranged for others to do it – a random bullet, an encounter with murderous thieves in the Bois."

"Never! She did nothing I would not have done – and will do in the future."

Chapter Ten

Once again in Paris, Bonaparte was, as he expected, the toast of the capital. With Josephine on his arm, disbursing her usual kindness and charm, Bonaparte attended the opera, the unveiling of monuments to his military victories and numerous public and private functions.

The news of the fleet's destruction had not yet reached Paris. When it did, he would have to manage that news somehow – or, better still, suppress it – if that could be done.

In the meantime, there was a political goal to achieve – one that required enormous skill in dissembling, plus courage of a different and more subtle kind than he had displayed on the battlefield. His goal was not a modest one. It was to become effectually the ruler of France without appearing to eliminate the republican form of government or arousing the opposition of the Directors, the legislature or the army. It was no small challenge.

Bonaparte turned to Talleyrand for strategic advice and to Josephine for a shrewd reaction to that advice based on her unfailingly sound instinct. He had been warned against trusting Talleyrand, and he had long believed that politics were not the province of women. Still, he listened carefully to these two very different advisors. He considered their counsel, but, ultimately, made his own decisions and planned his own campaign.

He knew the Directorate that governed France was growing increasingly unpopular. Once again, there were food shortages, public disorder and, without Bonaparte's generalship, consistent defeats on the battlefield. Both monarchist and radical revolutionary sentiment was increasing and becoming quite open. It was so open that the government seemed in serious jeopardy from both the left and the right; and the corrupt and inept Directorate seemed unable to prevent upheaval that could lead to return of the monarchy or of the "terror."

The most powerful Directors were Barras and Emanuel Sieyes. Playing the two against each other, Bonaparte sold them both on the idea of replacing the unpopular Directorate with a Consulate of three men. With subtle hints, he led each man to think he would be one of the three consuls, if not the most important of the three. Sieyes was so convinced of this that he began taking riding lessons, knowing that the French loved to see their leader on a horse.

At the time, there were two houses of the French legislature, the Council of Five Hundred and the Council of the Elders, the smaller, upper house. Bonaparte's brother Lucien was President of the Council of the Five Hundred.

To carry out his plan, Bonaparte directed Lucien to move both houses of the legislature temporarily to St. Cloud, some distance from Paris, using the excuse that the members of the legislature would otherwise be in danger.

At St. Cloud, Bonaparte reasoned, they would be isolated from any aroused Parisians, who might take to the streets to support one cause or another.

Once the legislators agreed to the move, Bonaparte issued invitations to each of the top French generals to join him for breakfast at Malmaison. Almost all attended, although they had no idea what was afoot. One by one, Bonaparte took them into his study. There, outlining his plan in a vague way that was not totally candid, he asked for their loyalty and support. Those waiting in the salon were soothed by Josephine's charm.

All but General Bernadotte agreed to support Bonaparte's plan, as they understood it. Bernadotte, a staunch republican, was uneasy about replacing the Directorate with a Consulate that, to Bernadotte, did not sound republican at all. He wanted no part of pressuring the legislature into adopting a new constitution that might jeopardize the Republic.

But Bernadotte was married to Desiree Clary, the sweetheart of Bonaparte's youth, and Desiree's sister, Julie, had married Bonaparte's brother Joseph. With Josephine's help, Joseph convinced Bernadotte to remain neutral and not to warn others of their plan.

Now, Bonaparte put the plan into operation. Accompanied by a select handful of generals, he rode into Paris, intending to convince Sieyes, one way or the other, to resign from the Directorate. Smiling, Sieyes quickly agreed, assuming, from his previous discussions with

Bonaparte, that he would become the principal executive of the new government.

Meanwhile, Talleyrand persuaded Barras to resign with surprising ease. Encountering no need to give Barras the bribe of 2 million francs he carried with him for that purpose, Talleyrand kept the money for himself.

With the resignation of the two key Directors' in hand, Bonaparte proceeded to St. Cloud, where the troops of his supporting generals ringed the temporary halls of the legislature. Bonaparte sent word to the delegates that they were in grave danger from a conspiracy that had just been unearthed and that the troops they saw were strictly for their protection.

When the proposal to end the Directorate was introduced in the legislature, it created a furor. Angry delegates, attired in the red togas symbolizing their office, shouted that the proponents of the measure were trying to destroy the Republic. Cries of "traitor," "bigot" and "fool" filled the hall. The heated debate continued for hours while Bonaparte waited at a distance with the troops. Finally, impatient and convinced that no action would ever be taken, Bonaparte took a bold and unprecedented step.

It was strictly forbidden for the military to enter a venue in which the legislature was meeting. Nevertheless, accompanied by three large grenadiers, Bonaparte burst into the meeting hall determined to bring matters to a head. He began by repeating that a conspiracy had placed the delegates in danger. This was greeted with enraged shouts of "shame!" and "oust him!" Then a deputy screamed "Name the conspirators – if there are any." Then others took up the cry "Yes, name the conspirators!" Still others began an even more ominous cry, shouting "Outlaw him! Outlaw him!" Soon, many were shouting for Bonaparte to be "outlawed," a status that could lead to the guillotine.

Suddenly, an enraged deputy rushed at Bonaparte brandishing a dagger. One of the grenadiers moved between the man and Bonaparte bravely taking the knife thrust in his own shoulder. He then disarmed the would be assassin. The three soldiers rushed Bonaparte through the mob of red togas to safety.

Within minutes, Lucien brought word to the generals and the officials accompanying them that the delegates had attempted to assassinate his brother and that a resolution had been offered to declare Bonaparte an "outlaw." He urged them to take quick and decisive action before that resolution passed. The generals agreed. The troops were ordered to advance into the meeting hall with fixed bayonets. Their orders were to force the delegates from the hall and from the entire area, so that they would not be likely to return for a further session.

Before a vote could be taken on the resolution to outlaw Bonaparte, the troops entered the hall, moving forward a step at a time, prodding at the delegates with their bayonets until they were forced outside. The threatening advance continued in the garden until the deputies shed the togas that hampered their movements and fled in every direction. When the troops had completed their assignment, the delegates' benches and the surrounding gardens were festooned with red togas. Not a delegate was in sight.

But, Lucien had informed a number of "reliable" delegates that they should enjoy their dinners and then return to the hall. Later, in an all night session, these loyal delegates passed a resolution ending the Directorate and establishing a provisional Consulate of three members to run the government. The provisional consuls were Bonaparte, Sieyes and Roger Ducos, who had supported Bonaparte's plan.

A new constitution was to be prepared by a special commission organized by the provisional Consulate. Later, the constitutional commission met, its membership arranged and dominated by Bonaparte. It created a new constitution providing for a "First Consul" with full executive power to run the country, plus two other Consuls who would be appointed by the First Consul and whose role would be strictly advisory.

Then, the commission voted on the First Consul. To the surprise of no one, except perhaps Sieyes, it was Bonaparte. Months later, a national plebiscite approved the new constitution and the new First Consul. By popular vote, Bonaparte was now in control of France.

Chapter Eleven

Bonaparte and Josephine left the house on the rue de la Victiore, moving first to the Luxembourg Palace and, later, to the Palace of the Tuilleries.

Bonaparte threw himself into the work of reorganizing and vitalizing the nation. He designated Talleyrand as Minister of Exterior Relations (i.e., foreign affairs) and the efficient, but somewhat sinister, Joseph Fouché as Minister of Police. Then, moving with his customary speed and working long hours, he began the changes that would shape France into the most dynamic and well organized nation in Europe.

Some changes were symbolic. The seven day week, with Sunday as a day of rest, was restored, as were the original names of the months. No longer were Parisians required to speak of "Brumaire," "Vendémiaire" and "Fructidor," as the revolutionary government had dictated.

Other changes were substantive. He created the highly centralized administration that has characterized the French government ever since. He created the Bank of France, reorganized the entire system of French education, as well as the judiciary, and designed the civil code in use not only in France, but in other countries and still called the "Code Napoleon" or "Napoleonic Code."

Despite his hard work and long hours, Bonaparte insisted on dining with Josephine; and, although he had the grand bedroom formerly occupied by Louis XVI, he slept every night with Josephine in her bedroom. Even during the day, he would stop to visit with her. He would explain the source of his tension, and she would soothe and comfort him.

Bonaparte created social changes as well. He barred Theresia Tallien and Julie Carreau from the palace, determined to restore morality and decency to public life and to make it clear that scandal would not be tolerated – unless, of course, it was created by the First Consul himself.

It was a time of great celebration. That winter, Parisians gave ten thousand balls and six thousand formal dinners. The latter could consist of as many as twenty-five courses, each matched with a wine of selected vintage. The women appeared in lavish gowns and tunics bedecked with diamonds. For the first time in years, there were, once again, servants in livery wearing powdered wigs.

Josephine would appear at such events, and she enjoyed them. But, unlike the others, she was almost always dressed in plain white satin, silk or muslin with small flowers in her hair, and always without expensive jewelry. She sought to be an example of the values and mores of the Republic; and to make it clear that she was "citizeness Bonaparte," not a queen.

Bonaparte and Josephine would often visit Malmaison, where they would walk hand in hand in Josephine's gardens and enjoy the company of those few friends of whom they were genuinely fond.

Perhaps, this time, the period of Bonaparte's First Consulate, was the happiest of their lives. Bonaparte had the work he loved and the power he had always wanted. Josephine had greater security than ever before. She had her gardens, plants and animals at Malmaison and a husband who, although busy recreating a nation and occasionally involving himself in an affair, basically continued to adore her.

CHAPTER TWELVE

FRANCE WAS STILL AT WAR IN EUROPE, with England, Russia and Austria arrayed against her. Without Bonaparte's generalship, the army of the Republic had experienced defeats, but no significant victories. Bonaparte determined to take the field himself, but to do so secretly in order to avoid creating public alarm or encouraging plots by royalists or radical revolutionaries. He knew the secret could not be kept for long, but perhaps he could achieve a major victory before the plotting became too dangerous.

So, one spring day, he left Paris quietly at dawn, heading not for the European front but for Italy. There, in another of his extraordinary military strikes, he led a French army through an alpine pass into the heart of enemy territory, attacking the Austrians from their lightly guarded rear, creating chaos and panic in Vienna. The Austrians desperately counter-attacked. At Marengo, after a fierce battle, Bonaparte threw French reinforcements into the fray at a critical time, the Austrians fled and another great victory was won.

After the battle, Bonaparte's chef came to his tent almost in tears. "General, I am desolate. There is no cream with which to lighten the sauce for your chicken."

"What do you have?"

"Only tomatoes and garlic, General."

"That will do splendidly."

And Chicken Marengo was born.

As a result of reverses suffered by the French in the early phases of Marengo, the rumor spread that the army had been defeated and Bonaparte killed. The rumor reached the Palace just as Josephine was giving a reception for a number of foreign diplomats and government officials. She turned white and thought that she would faint. She stepped away, leaning against a column. After a moment, however, she caught her breath and returned to her guests, still pale and shaking.

At that moment, a servant announced the arrival of a military courier fresh from the front. Exhausted, the man entered, his uniform stained with sweat and mud.

"Citizeness, these were sent to you by First Consul Bonaparte."

Unwrapping a large canvas wrapped parcel, he laid captured Austrian battle flags at her feet.

"He has won a great victory."

"And the First Consul, himself, is he well?" she asked in a quiet voice.

"Couldn't be better, Madame. Couldn't be better."

CHAPTER THIRTEEN

WHILE RECREATING FRANCE in a more efficient and productive way, Bonaparte took a number of steps to preserve his own position. One measure was to bring back Catholicism as the established religion of the state. Churches that had been closed or re-designated "Temples of Reason" were reopened. The rue Honore was once again the rue St. Honore. Masses were once again conducted and Parisians heard the magnificent sound of church bells throughout the city, including the deep throated bell of Notre Dame.

Hearing the citywide ringing of bells at breakfast, Josephine smiled at her husband.

"My God, how the French love the Church. You've given them great joy by restoring it."

Bonaparte's face became serious. "I didn't do it for them. I did it for me. It is one thing to become the leader of a nation. It is quite another to remain the leader. I mean to remain. By bringing back the church, I take away a powerful argument of the royalists who would overthrow me. I buy support from the Pope who, even without armies, has significant power. And, as you point out, my dearest, I make the people happy. If their lives are harsh, they can look forward to the afterlife. If they are mistreated or encounter cruelty, they can turn the other cheek, rather than start a revolution.

"I'm also going to establish a program of amnesty for

aristocrats who left France because of the revolution – at least those who did not actually fight against us in some foreign army. That will also defang the royalist movement."

Bonaparte pointed to her with a smile, "I want you to be my 'commissioner' to pass upon who gets amnesty and who does not."

"Why me?"

"Because I trust you, and because the aristocrats think of you as almost one of them. After all, you were married to Alexandre de Beauharnais, who *was* one of them."

"And you think these measures will help you to stay?"

"Those and many others. I do not intend to relinquish my responsibilities . . . ever."

"My darling Bonaparte, you begin to talk like a king."

"Well, Citizeness Bonaparte, it may come to that."

CHAPTER FOURTEEN

BONAPARTE'S AMNESTY POLICY was successful on two levels. First, numerous aristocrats who had emigrated and languished in other countries enthusiastically flooded back to France, depriving Louis XVIII of valuable support. Louis, who became the theoretical "King of France" on the execution of Louis XVI and his son, was now in exile in Poland. He realized that his cause was seriously weakened by Bonaparte's amnesty and also by his restoration of the church.

On a second level, the amnesty gave Josephine enormous stature and importance among the aristocratic émigrés whose return she had approved and often arranged, even when opposed by others in the government. Many who, years before, would have shunned her, became her grateful friends.

Misperceiving Bonaparte's policies as evincing a genuine embrace of the royalist cause, Louis XVIII sent out a feeler. He wrote Bonaparte suggesting that he use his formidable sword to restore the Bourbon Monarchy, hinting that Bonaparte would be richly rewarded and would play a major role in the restored royal government.

Bonaparte's policies had, of course, been in his own interests, not those of Louis. He was well aware that appearing to favor the royalist cause would be unpopular. Adroit politician that he was, he replied to Louis that, if he hoped to re-ascend the throne of France he would have to march into Paris over the bodies of one hundred thousand Frenchmen, including that of Napoleon Bonaparte.

Naturally, Bonaparte and Fouché made sure that his letter was published in every newspaper in France.

Reading the letter in his Polish court in exile, Louis got the point. "This man," he bellowed, "wants to be king himself. It is now plain from his policies and from this letter. Between the lines it says 'My policies are designed to put me on the throne, not you.' Something must be done about him!"

Hearing these words, two of Louis' most efficient operatives nodded to each other and left the room.

On Christmas eve, Bonaparte, Josephine and Hortense were dressed to attend the first performance of Hayden's "Creation" at the Paris Opera House. Josephine emerged from the Palace wearing one of the cashmere shawls that had become her trademark, used to cover the clinging gowns she wore beneath them.

Bonaparte, who always took an avid interest in his wife's attire, objected that the shawl did not match her dress. She returned with Hortense to change the shawl, while he proceeded to the opera in a smaller coach, leaving the larger royal coach to the women.

After changing, Josephine and Hortense set out for the opera in the royal coach. As they entered the rue Nicaise, they were thrown from the coach by a huge explosion. Shaken and slightly somewhat bloodied, Josephine turned to the commander of their military escort.

"What happened Captain?"

"A bomb, madame. A very powerful bomb. Obviously meant for the First Consul. Look about you. The street is littered with the dead and wounded. You have some blood on your dress. May I escort you home?"

"No, Captain, we will proceed to the opera. The First Consul is already there and will be concerned."

Meanwhile, Bonaparte was already in his box at the opera and growing impatient. When Josephine and Hortense arrived and told him what had occurred, he immediately ordered that an announcement be made from the stage. The opera manager stepped in front of the curtain.

"I have an important announcement. There had been an attempt to assassinate the First Consul. Fortunately, he has arrived here safely with his wife and family." As the manager gestured to the royal box, the crowd stood cheering wildly. Napoleon rose, delighting the crowd with a crisp military salute.

The next morning, an angry Bonaparte met with Fouché, his Minister of Police. Bonaparte had escaped death, but the bombs had killed and wounded fifty-two people; and there would be more such attempts. He demanded that Fouché find the guilty men, who he believed were radical revolutionaries enraged over his policy of amnesty for the aristocrats.

"No, First Consul" Fouché replied. "It was the royalists themselves. Your policies have rendered them far less potent. Besides, they believe you want to be king yourself, which could be the death of the Bourbon cause."

"King myself – preposterous!" Bonaparte was not ready to admit such thoughts to anyone but Josephine.

Later that day, he met with Talleyrand. He was ready to send up a trial balloon.

"Fouché says that the royalists believe I could become king. I said 'that's preposterous.'" Leaning on Bonaparte's massive desk, Talleyrand smiled.

"It is not preposterous at all. Did you fail to hear the cheering at the opera. Your popularity is enormous. Most of the public would not object to your position becoming permanent. And, if it was permanent, how different would that be from being king?"

Ultimately, Fouché proved correct. A thorough investigation and a bit of torture showed that the bomb was the work of enraged royalists. Royalist fanatics involved in the assassination plot were quickly arrested and guillotined.

Chapter Fifteen

JOSEPHINE SAT AT LUNCH with her old friend Violet de Kreny. Violet, never shy, commented on what appeared to be a note of sadness in Josephine.

"I do have some concerns, Violet."

"I hope you don't let the rumors of Bonaparte's occasional affairs sadden you. You know that his sister, Pauline, encourages them. She introduces him to every pretty girl she can find, virtually pushes them into his bed. She despises you."

Josephine smiled at her friend's extraordinary candor, although Bonaparte's dalliances with actresses and dancers were no secret.

"No, it's not that – and I know about Pauline. What tears at me is our inability to produce a child, something he wants so badly."

"Of course, the 'male heir' – the man's practically a king. His thoughts would, of course, turn to that subject and wonder if you can bear a child."

Josephine was startled that Violet would guess at what was in her husband's mind. She determined to protect his secret.

"Oh no. Bonaparte has no royal ambitions. Besides, it may not be my fault that we have no children. I do have two children already."

"Yes, and they are lovely children. But, my dear, you were much younger then."

Chapter Sixteen

For a moment, marriages competed with governing for Bonaparte's attention. In a civil service, his sister Caroline married General Murat, the huge cavalry officer and ferocious fighter on whom Bonaparte so often had relied. Hoping that it would soften the family's hatred of her, Josephine had convinced an unwilling Bonaparte to consent to the match.

Next, Bonaparte insisted that Hortense, Josephine's slender blonde daughter, marry his brother Louis, who, although intelligent, was emotionally unstable and was suffering from gonorrhea. Hortense was miserable at the prospect, but realized that the match might enhance her mother's position with the Bonaparte family. And, since Hortense suspected that Bonaparte had royal ambitions, she hoped her marriage would produce the "male heir," reducing the likelihood of Bonaparte's contemplating divorce – a possibility Hortense recognized and feared.

Sacrificing her own future for her mother's welfare, Hortense agreed to the match. The rest of the Bonaparte family was furious. Obviously, in terms of inheritance as well as potential succession to the throne (something they too speculated about), a child of Louis and Hortense would be Bonaparte's likely heir, rather than any of the rest of them or their children.

Caroline raged. Married to Murat, she had intended her own child to be the heir. Now that chance was gone.

Hortense had trumped Caroline's marriage to Bonaparte's friend and key officer with a marriage to his brother.

Lucien, also embittered by the decision, spread the rumor that Hortense was Bonaparte's lover and was pregnant with his child. Lucien confided this to Louis in hopes of convincing him to cancel the marriage.

"He can't get a child on the Creole whore, so he does the next best thing – he fucks her daughter."

Although full of paranoid tendencies, Louis failed to take the bait.

"Lucien, that's insane. Hortense cares nothing for me and, for that matter, I care nothing for her. But she is not and has never been in our brother's bed. Never! I would stake my life on it."

"In fact, Louis, you are."

For the wedding, the salon of the rue de la Victoire house had been converted to a chapel. This was to be a formal, religious ceremony.

A pale, red-eyed Hortense knelt beside Louis. At the same time, Murat and Caroline knelt before the priest so that their own civil marriage could be sanctified by the church.

Josephine quietly asked if Bonaparte wished to join his siblings in this, making their own marriage binding in the eyes of the church. When Bonaparte softly but firmly declined, she experienced a frisson of fear – a fear that, from that point, never left her. She knew Bonaparte loved her. She was sure of it. But he was plainly avoiding any action that could frustrate his obtaining a divorce.

Her fear was enhanced by Bonaparte's new civil code. Although, in other areas, it simplified and enforced moral values, it continued the concept of liberalized divorce. Was this another sign that Bonaparte was keeping that option open for himself?

Josephine feared it was.

Chapter Seventeen

Bonaparte's accomplishments were now widely recognized throughout the nation. He had forced every country but England to withdraw from the fight against France. Now, even the English had signed a treaty of peace. For the first time since the revolution, France was not at war.

And the peace was accompanied by political and economic well being. Bonaparte had stabilized the franc, his civil code had brought predictability and rationality to the law, his rebuilt educational system was thriving and the country was experiencing prosperity for the first time in many years.

Talleyrand suggested that it was a good time for Bonaparte to become "Counsel for Life," as a tactical step toward the throne and one that could still be perceived as "republican." Bonaparte approved, and the legislature conferred that unique title on him. Of course, it had little choice. The public enthusiastically approved the new title. Bonaparte was their idol. Heroic pictures of him were in every home, shop and school.

What was less widely recognized than Bonaparte's becoming "Counsel for Life," was that the same legislature quietly added the principle of heredity to the constitution. Bonaparte's heir, if he had one, would inherit his title and position.

When Josephine realized this, she became profoundly

depressed. Every move Bonaparte made seemed to create an even greater possibility that he would someday discard her in his need for an heir. She remained confident of his love, but she knew the man well and knew that love could be outweighed by the quest for power, which he rationalized as serving the interests of France.

She vowed to stave off divorce as best she could by giving Bonaparte as much support, sweetness and joy as possible.

She arranged for them to spend more time together at Malmaison. They relished the small, comfortable rooms and the lush, informal gardens, which Josephine supplemented with her growing collection of exotic flowers, plants and herbs.

They would invite young friends over for weekends, playing wild children's games on the extensive lawn, hiding behind the ancient trees and chasing each other up the garden paths.

And, each night, they would lie in each other arms, usually in Josephine's dramatically tented bed.

Any observer would have believed their relationship at this time was perfect. But most observers could not perceive the cloud that hung over Josephine's ability to enjoy that seemingly ideal relationship.

Chapter Eighteen

While he treasured his time with Josephine at Malmaison, Bonaparte began to organize a "court" at the Tuilleries Palace with protocol much like that of a king.

The curtsy was reintroduced, and Bonaparte's sisters were subjected to the indignity of having to rise when Josephine entered the room. There were frequent receptions and balls at the Palace at which Josephine won the admiration of their guests with her extraordinary grace and charm.

Weekly formal dinners were also given. Guests would enter between files of soldiers in dress uniforms, while a band played martial tunes. When the guests were seated in the dining area, Bonaparte and Josephine would make a formal entrance and be seated at a table for two on a raised dais.

Foreign ambassadors would invariably report to their governments on Josephine's ability to win over everyone in attendance and on her attire. No longer appearing in the simple costumes of Citizeness Bonaparte, she now wore gowns that were spectacular in their design and ingenuity, often being sewn with precious jewels, silver or gold stars or even rose petals.

Despite the success of their public lives and the pleasures of their moments together at Malmaison, Bonaparte became more open and less discreet in his liaisons with other women, particularly young actresses and dancers. He felt that, as one who had the status of a king, he should behave like one. After all, didn't all kings have mistresses?

When, on rare occasions, Josephine complained, Bonaparte assured her that these were short term affairs involving no element of love, and that she was his only, his eternal love.

Josephine was hardly mollified by these rationalizations, so common to adulterous husbands; but, in her determination to remain sweet and supportive, she tried to bear this painful situation. She considered divorce a far greater danger than adultery.

CHAPTER NINETEEN

AS HE BECAME MORE AND MORE COMMITTED to living as if he were royal, Bonaparte seemed less and less committed to peace. He publicly insulted the British ambassador in the crudest possible manner, leading to abolition of the treaty between the two nations and, ultimately, a declaration of war by England's King George III.

Bonaparte left for the Channel coast to prepare an invasion of England. If he could only land his army on the English coast, he was certain he could take London in a matter of days. The trick, of course, was getting the army across the channel without having it destroyed by the British Fleet. That remained the problem year after year, and the invasion never materialized.

Meanwhile, Bonaparte was having trouble with his always difficult family and particularly with his sister Pauline. At the time of his marriage to Josephine, Pauline had said proudly that she "could do everything Josephine could do – including satisfy lovers. It is just that Josephine has had much more experience at such things."

Now Pauline was living up to her pronouncement and even exceeding it.

Hearing from Fouché that Pauline had spent three days and nights in her bedroom with General Macdonald and that she was involved in a tawdry affair with some young officers, Bonaparte ordered one of the officers named by Fouché to report to him.

He began by trying to put the officer at ease.

"Captain, I intend you no harm, but only to ascertain the true situation regarding my sister. You may speak freely without fear. Has my sister been behaving in a licentious manner?"

"May I speak candidly, First Consul?"

"Absolutely."

"For a week, five of us shared a house with Pauline. During the day and most of the night, she would bed one, two or even three of us at a time. Each of us enjoyed her favors at least once a day, often twice. Frankly, First Consul, she was the greatest tramp imaginable and the most desirable."

Within a week, Pauline was ordered to accompany her husband, General Leclerc to Santo Domingo where, months later, he died of yellow fever.

Chapter Twenty

Talleyrand now began to assure Bonaparte that it was wiser to become, rather than merely to act, royal. If Bonaparte was ready to take that next, critical step, Talleyrand advised use of the term "Emperor," rather than "King," since the latter expression had become synonymous with evil during the revolution.

Talleyrand became even more open in advocating divorce, so that the Emperor could have an heir and establish a permanent royal line. Talleyrand argued that, if Bonaparte became Emperor, an heir would make him a far less appealing target for assassination. Smiling slyly and pointing his finger at Bonaparte like a pistol, the former Bishop explained,

"Kill you as you are now, and there is no one to succeed you. The conspirators could take over the government with ease. Kill you after you have an heir recognized by the public, and the nation would not allow the conspirators to take over. They would support the succession of your legitimate heir. Ergo, First Consul, conspirators would necessarily be less inclined to try assassination if you had an heir."

Bonaparte followed and accepted this logic. But there were problems with divorce as a solution. Although he didn't explain this to Talleyrand, his problems were twofold. First, he still loved and felt he needed Josephine. Second, even if he concluded that he must have a divorce, how could he ever bring himself to tell her?

Meanwhile, Talleyrand and Bonaparte also discussed which of the Bourbons posed a realistic threat of uniting the royalists and the public to the point at which they might try to overthrow Bonaparte should he become Emperor.

Talleyrand presented his shrewd analysis leaning on Bonaparte's desk.

"Fat, indolent Louis XVIII rotting with gout in a Polish exile could never inspire a popular movement. Nor could his foppish younger brother in exile in England. Those are not men to lead a revolution."

"But," Talleyrand continued, "there is such a man . . . the Duke of Enghien. He is handsome, intelligent and directly in the Bourbon royal line. Enghien is thirty-two, strong, brave and well spoken. With respect, your excellency, should the economy turn weak or prices too high or our enemies win some major victory, or should your being named Emperor, in itself, create public discontent, Enghien is a man who could lead an uprising that could create serious problems for us. What is more, we are certain that he is conspiring with the English and French royalist agents to do just that."

"Where is Enghien now?"

"Just across the border in Baden."

"What do you suggest, Talleyrand?"

"Our people could easily bring him across the border to justice."

"To justice?"

"I believe your excellency knows what I mean."

Bonaparte rose and spun the huge globe that stood near his desk. Then he turned back to Talleyrand.

"Very well, see that it is done."

Two weeks later, a detachment of specially selected French troops slipped across the border under cover of night. Through local spies, they located Enghein walking to his fiancée's home accompanied by his dog. He was quickly captured, rushed across the border to France and thrown in a prison cell.

Hearing of Enghien's kidnaping, Josephine rushed to Bonaparte's office, determined to convince him to spare the man.

"Bonaparte, Talleyrand is wrong. Killing this young man is a serious mistake. The stain of this crime will follow you forever!"

"My dear, you are loveliest when aroused, and your soft feminine thoughts are a credit to you. But this is an issue of realpolitik, not a matter for the soft heart of a woman – even one I love. Besides, the man is in league with spies. He poses a grave danger to the nation."

"That's what the English said about Mary Stewart before they beheaded her."

"Well, they were right."

Josephine continued to plead for Enghien's life, but to no avail. Within hours, the Duke was marched to an open field, where he faced a French firing squad. After gently handing his dog to a French officer, he was shot to death.

Three weeks later, the senate, totally under Bonaparte's control, voted unanimously that he be declared "Emperor of the French."

Chapter Twenty-One

Most Frenchmen thrilled to the idea that their heroic First Consul was now to be their Emperor. Church bells rang and cannons were fired in salute of the new monarch. A national plebiscite endorsed Bonaparte's becoming Emperor by a huge majority.

But the enthusiasm of the Bonaparte family was lessened by squabbling over their own titles and positions. While Joseph and Louis were each given the title of "prince," making Hortense a "princess," Caroline and Elisa were enraged at this and at the fact that they remained without any royal title.

Conscious of the family's modest roots, Bonaparte considered their claims absurd. Sarcastically, he told his sisters "Anyone would think I had robbed you of the inheritance of the late king, our father."

Still, the two sisters' rage continued and grew. Finally, Bonaparte, unable to bear their fury, allowed the two to be addressed as "Imperial Highness," a title he also conferred on Pauline, who, returning from her exile in Santo Domingo, had married Prince Borghese of Rome. Borghese's title was an ancient one, and, as "Princess Pauline Borghese," she was less concerned with acquiring newly minted French titles handed out by her brother.

Bonaparte took personal charge of every detail of his coronation. It was to be attended only by the upper classes. He would not be crowned before "twenty thousand fishwives." It would be in Notre Dame; and, despite the protests of his family, Josephine was to be crowned "Empress."

The family and others argued that, with rare exceptions, the wives of kings had not been crowned, not even Marie Antoinette.

But, whatever his private thoughts, Bonaparte was unmovable on the point. He lectured his family and other skeptics. "It is only fair that she should now be an Empress. If I had been thrown in prison, instead of ascending a throne, she would have shared my misfortune. It is only right that, now, she should share my grandeur! Yes, she will be crowned!"

Despite such unequivocal statements, however, his doubts persisted. Pressed on the point by Talleyrand, he had decided that, ultimately, he must divorce her. But, while he could lead the charge at Arcola in the face of murderous enemy fire, he lacked the courage to tell Josephine that they must divorce. He tried to persuade first Eugene and then Hortense to deliver the bad news to their mother, and both flatly refused. They would render any other service to Bonaparte – just not that one.

Of course, Josephine knew that Bonaparte was entertaining thoughts of divorce. Bonaparte guessed that she knew. But that was not the same as telling her.

From time to time, he wavered on the subject of crowning her Empress. Talleyrand argued that, if there was to be a divorce, casting off an empress, rather than just a wife, might not sit well with the public. Bonaparte saw the logic of that position, but, each time he considered the matter, he came back to the fact that she had shared the pitfalls of his life, always remaining sweet and supportive and that he still deeply loved her.

One evening, having suggested to his family that he was reconsidering the matter of crowning Josephine, he was so enraged by his sisters' expressions of gloating triumph, that, in a state of high emotion, he rushed to Josephine's bedroom, took her in his arms and, stroking her as he would a child, said the words she hoped to hear.

"The pope will be here at the end of the month. He will crown us both. Start to prepare for the ceremony."

Chapter Twenty-Two

The Pope did arrive in Paris, where he was overwhelmed by the number of Parisians seeking a papal audience. He had brought with him only a small number of religious medals and rosaries which he could bless and give to those who came before him. Soon, he was blessing eyeglasses, family portraits, tennis rackets and numerous other items presented by newly devout Parisians.

The day before the coronation, Josephine had a lengthy audience with the Pope. When she confessed that her marriage to Bonaparte had been a civil one only, he told her that, much as he would like to follow the Emperor's wishes and her own, he simply could not crown and announce as Empress a woman unmarried in the eyes of the church and thus living in sin. He would make many compromises to please the Emperor, but not this one. This one would be impossible.

Josephine was, of course, distraught; and, when Bonaparte heard of the Pope's decision, he took a step that seemed wholly inconsistent with Talleyrand's advice and with his own previous doubts and plans. He quickly arranged for a midnight Catholic wedding, and the two were married at a temporary alter erected in his study. The religious service was conducted by Bonaparte's Uncle Fesch, a crude and fleshy priest who, as Letizia Bonaparte's stepbrother, had been made a cardinal and had gained considerable wealth from government contracts. Regardless of the shortcomings of Uncle Fesch, however, Bonaparte and Josephine were now firmly and formally married in the eyes of the church. Her coronation could proceed, and she gained renewed hope that perhaps Bonaparte might not press her for a divorce after all.

Chapter Twenty-Three

THE DAY OF THE CORONATION was one of the coldest in memory. The sky was dark grey. Snow lay on the rooftops, and the streets were icy. Still, Parisians lined the route leading from the Tuilleries to Notre Dame. They were held back by row upon row of armed soldiers, frost forming on their greatcoats.

In the Tuilleries Palace the action had started long before dawn. Josephine's costumer arrived at sunrise to begin the process of making up her face. Many of the ladies had slept sitting up in chairs so as not to mess their hair done the night before. Still, there was much to be done, and the preparations were significantly behind schedule.

The Pope and coaches full of Cardinals and Bishops left the Tuilleries on time, as did the state coaches bearing richly attired dignitaries and generals in full dress uniform. Before each coach trotted a detachment of cavalry, brilliantly attired in silver chest plates and helmets with long horsehair plumes.

Bonaparte was very late. As always, Josephine waited patiently for him. She was in white satin with a gold veil embroidered with the Emperor's bee symbol. She wore diamonds every place diamonds could be worn.

By the time Bonaparte finally appeared in the bizarre, diamond encrusted costume designed for the occasion, the event was almost two hours late. Now, as cannons roared and church bells rang out, the royal coach clattered down the streets lined with shivering Parisians.

Talleyrand was concerned that there seemed more cheering for Josephine than for Bonaparte. But he knew such things are difficult to measure; and, even if it was true, he saw that Bonaparte did not seem to mind. It was his day, and he was cheerful despite the cold and without regard to which of the two was cheered more enthusiastically.

As Bonaparte and Josephine descended from their coach in front of the great cathedral, the sun broke through the clouds, creating a magic moment. Bonaparte turned to Josephine who gave him a radiant smile, as the crowd cheered wildly.

The interior of the cathedral was bitter cold. Most of the assembled crowd had been waiting for hours, including even the Pope who sat patiently, seemingly in prayer. Their long frigid wait was still not over. The Emperor and Empress were now to change from their traveling costumes into their coronation attire. They were led to a robing room for this purpose.

An hour later, Bonaparte finally appeared wearing a floor length satin robe, over which was an ermine-lined purple velvet mantle embroidered with his bee symbol. The train of his mantle was borne by his two brothers and the second and third consuls. On his head was a gold laurel wreath.

Then Josephine appeared wearing a similar gown and mantle with a train borne by the three Bonaparte sisters and two sisters-in-law, now all "princesses." On Josephine's head was a diadem blazing with diamonds.

They were preceded by officials bearing their crowns, as well as the Emperor's sword, ring and royal orb.

Josephine was radiant and completely at ease. Bonaparte was relaxed and quite pleased with the proceedings except that, at one point, believing that the procession was moving too slowly, he prodded Uncle Fesch in the back with his scepter. It was, after all, his coronation and he would set the pace – as he had done the entire day.

The imperial pair advanced up the aisle to the two thrones placed before the alter, at which point, they knelt briefly to pray. Then, while they remained kneeling, the Pope anointed the two with holy oil.

Next came the surprise Bonaparte had planned without telling anyone. As the Pope moved to pick up the two crowns to place them on the heads of the Imperial pair, Bonaparte moved more quickly. Lifting the Imperial crown high in the air, he placed it on his own head. The message was clear – he wore the Imperial crown by his own right, not by permission of the Pope or anyone else.

Now, Bonaparte picked up Josephine's crown and moved toward her. She moved toward him in response. As she knelt before him, he placed her crown first on his own head, then, lifting it again, placed it on her head, doing so in almost a playful manner, backing away and appraising it carefully for a moment as it sat on her head, then lifting it and readjusting it as if carefully positioning a new hat.

At this moment, they looked at each other as if their love was eternal and nothing short of death could ever part them.

After receiving their crowns, the two ascended their thrones. This led to a small contretemps as Caroline and Elisa dropped Josephine's train, throwing her seriously off balance as she stepped upwards toward the throne. Caroline had been holding smelling salts to her nose throughout the ceremony, as if she was in danger of fainting, while Elisa's face was a sullen mask. Plainly, dropping the train was a deliberate act.

A scowling Bonaparte took a step in their direction, as if to smite them with the Imperial sword. Angrily he hissed "pick that up – *now*!"

Sheepishly, the sisters complied. A stern look from the Emperor quickly silenced the titter that went through those spectators close enough to witness the incident.

Now the Pope cried out, "*Vivat Imperator in aeternum!*" He returned to the alter as the presiding officers of the senate administered the civil oath of office.

Once again, Notre Dame's great bell sounded and cannons were fired, as Bonaparte and Josephine, proceeded by their entourage, left the cathedral. They were now, formally, Emperor and Empress of the French.

That night, once again defying tradition, Bonaparte insisted on dining alone with Josephine. During dinner, he asked her to wear her crown "because it is so becoming, and you look so pretty in it. No one could wear a crown with more grace."

After dinner, they returned to Josephine's bedroom where they spent the night in each others arms.

* * * *

Louis David took years to complete his famous painting of the coronation, carefully portraying all of the significant figures in attendance. Some changes were required. Bonaparte insisted that his mother, who had not attended the ceremony, be painted in, and that his sisters not be shown bearing Josephine's train lest it recall the unfortunate moment when they dropped it.

Bonaparte thanked David "for recording for posterity the proof of the affection I wished to give the woman who shares with me the burden of office."

Chapter Twenty-Four

After the coronation, Bonaparte and Josephine plunged into a vast array of formal engagements and tours. On the way to Bonaparte's added coronation as King of Lombardy, they visited the battlefields of his earlier Italian campaigns. Josephine was an interested and enthusiastic listener to his moment by moment depiction of the battles he had won and the tactics he had employed to win them.

The coronation in Lombardy was solely for Bonaparte, although Josephine automatically became Queen of Lombardy. Bonaparte was in a playful mood. He strode down the aisle of the cathedral with the crown of Lombardy tucked carelessly under his arm like some insignificant package. After the ceremony, he chased Josephine around their bedroom trying to tickle her until, exhausted from laughing, she begged him to stop.

When Bonaparte left Josephine once again to inspect the preparations for an invasion of England, he wrote her more of his loving and erotic letters, relating his desolation that "my sweet Josephine is missing" and promising to give her "a thousand affectionate kisses *everywhere*."

The invasion of England could not proceed, because the French fleet under Admiral Villeneuve remained in the harbor of Cadiz, boxed in by the more competent and aggressive British Navy.

Meanwhile, the Austrians were preparing to renew the war against France in alliance with the British, the Russians and perhaps the Prussians as well. Bonaparte decided on a swift movement across Europe to strike a decisive blow against the Austrians and Russians before they could join forces and be prepared to fight. Then he would speed back to the Channel Coast to deal with the English.

At her entreaty, Bonaparte took Josephine with him as far as Strasbourg. "You may come along, my dearest, but you must travel as I do – swiftly and with little comfort." She agreed, and, true to his word, they covered the distance by coach in four and a half days, stopping only for a quick change of horses.

Leaving an exhausted Josephine in richly appointed quarters in Strasbourg, Bonaparte personally led his army eastward. As was his custom, his troops lived off the land, taking meat, eggs and vegetables from farms along the way.

At Ulm, the Austrians were caught completely off guard before they were joined by the Russians and while they still believed Bonaparte was on the Channel Coast. In a short engagement, most of the Austrian army was destroyed with very few French losses. The victory was overwhelming.

But it was overshadowed by some very bad news. Shortly after the battle at Ulm, an exhausted naval officer was brought to Bonaparte, his uniform stained with mud and streaked with sweat. He had ridden non-stop from the Coast. The officer reported that Admiral Villeneuve had finally taken the French fleet out of Cadiz, but that it had been utterly destroyed by Nelson in a battle off

Cape Trafalgar. "The man is a devil," the officer said. "He violated every principle of naval warfare. Instead of laying his ships alongside ours, so that he could bring all of his guns to bear, he formed his fleet into two lines perpendicular to our fleet and he sailed those two lines into the port side of our formation."

The officer paused for a sip of coffee. "Of course, this allowed us to bring all of our port guns to bear on the unprotected bows of his ships as they approached our formation. Unfortunately, the sea was rough and our gunners were unable to time their broadsides effectively as their ships rolled high, then low.

"Soon the two lines of British ships penetrated our formation, cutting off the forward elements of our fleet from those in the rear and placing the British ships so that their port and starboard guns could fire broadside after broadside at the unprotected bows and sterns of our ships, while receiving very little return fire.

"The lead elements of our fleet had to travel a great distance in order to turn around and sail back to the battle. By that time, almost all of the ships in the rear of our formation had been destroyed. Then, the British fell upon the returning lead elements of our fleet and destroyed them too.

"The only good news, sire, is that Nelson was killed on the deck of his flagship as she approached our formation. Our snipers got him."

Bonaparte glared at the young officer. "It can hardly be called 'good news' when a brave and ingenious commander has fallen. Go have some dinner, son. You've had a long, hard ride."

Standing there on an Austrian hill, Bonaparte thought of Nelson and removed his hat out of respect. Here was a man who fought as I do. Always bold, always surprising, always brave. He turned in the direction of the sea and was silent.

Now, of course, an invasion of England was impossible. Bonaparte badly needed a quick and major victory to bring the Russians to the peace table before the Prussians, emboldened by the news of Trafalgar, joined the alliance.

As winter approached, Bonaparte and his army pursued the Russians and Austrians through the snow and rain day after day, seeking a conclusive battle. Finally, with his army exhausted and outnumbered, he caught the allies near a place called Austerlitz. Bonaparte's chief of staff rode up to him as he surveyed the field. He pointed to a ridge of high ground across the valley. "We must occupy those heights, Sire, before the enemy does. We must, of course, seize the high ground."

'Seize the high ground,' Bonaparte thought. Yes, every military manual tells you that this is what you must do. Then he smiled as he thought of Nelson.

"If we occupy those heights, the enemy will not fight. They'll continue to maneuver until we're even more depleted and exhausted. No, we'll allow the Russian to take the high ground. Then they'll feel confident. Then they'll fight.

"Thin out our right, so that it appears vulnerable. Place most of our visible strength on the left. And send Marshal Davout to me."

By now, Bonaparte had made his key generals into "Marshals" giving them elaborate batons denoting their new rank.

As Bonaparte planned, when the Russians arrived, they immediately occupied the high ground. Their officers were amazed that Bonaparte had made the classic blunder of not doing so, since he had been first on the field.

The Tsar, Alexander I, was a tall and handsome young man, courageous but inexperienced in battle. He quickly saw the weakness of the French right and ordered his men to form up for an immediate attack on that vulnerable point.

General Kutuzov, a battle tested old warrior, urged the Tsar not to attack.

"Why?" queried the Tsar.

"Because it doesn't feel right."

"That's not a reason, Kutuzov."

"In battle, Sire, feelings can be more important than reason, and, I repeat, this does not feel right."

But the young Tsar turned away and ordered an immediate full scale attack on the French right. The Russian troops poured down from the high ground, their bayonets fixed, charging straight at the seemingly weak French right. When they were 50 yards from their goal, the sun burst through the clouds, and two added regiments of French riflemen, previously hidden in the fog, stepped forward into line on the French right. Commanded by Marshal Davout, they added considerable strength to what had appeared the weak side of Bonaparte's force.

The Russians were caught in a murderous fire. Their advance slowed, then halted. The survivors began moving back toward the uphill slopes down which they had charged so boldly only a few minutes before.

But much had happened during their downhill attack. As his right was reinforced, Bonaparte had ordered his powerful left wing to circle around behind the heights, ready to mount an attack on the lightly defended ridge.

Kutuzov saw this maneuver as it was developing and persuaded the Tsar to flee to the rear before they were completely encircled. They left not a moment too soon. The shouting troops of Bonaparte's left rushed the heights from the rear before the Russian cannon could even be turned in their direction.

Now, the main body of the Russian force was hopelessly pinned between the French behind them on the heights and the reinforced French right that faced them in the valley.

Volley after volley of rifle and cannon fire poured into their ranks from before and behind them. Those Russians troops still alive tried to save themselves by retreating over a frozen lake that lay near the battlefield. Bonaparte, determined to end the allied threat once and for all, directed his guns to fire red hot cannon balls onto the ice covering the lake. Soon the ice cracked and then collapsed into the water, drowning thousands of escaping Russians.

The victory was complete and devastating. Without the support of the Russian armies, the Austrians sued for peace. Contrary to the advice of Talleyrand, Bonaparte imposed extremely harsh terms, including the loss of significant Austrian territory and, most importantly, abolition of the centuries old Holy Roman Empire. From now on, there would be no Holy Roman Emperor, merely an "Emperor of Austria," with an "empire" embarrassingly small. Bonaparte was now the master of Europe, having defeated the combination of every other major European power.

One territory forfeited by the Austrians was Bavaria. Seizing the opportunity to bind the newly appropriated land to his personal reign, Bonaparte immediately arranged for the marriage of Josephine's son, Eugene to Princess Augusta, the daughter of the Elector of Bavaria.

He wrote Josephine asking her to join him in Munich for the wedding. She, of course, accepted and, on her progress was unanimously lauded for her extraordinary charm. As Bonaparte put it, "I win battles, but Josephine wins hearts." He was proud of her and he told her so.

When Bonaparte arrived in Munich, he encountered serious obstacles to his plans for Eugene's wedding. For one, the prospective bride was already engaged to the Crown Prince of Baden and was determined to marry him.

Moreover, the bride's father found Eugene insufficiently royal or even noble, adding that he was really nothing more than "a French gentleman."

Bonaparte quickly solved these problems.

Pronouncing Eugene a "fearless, blameless knight," Bonaparte adopted him as his own son, made him Viceroy of Italy and conferred upon him the title "Imperial Highness." As an added inducement, the bride's father was promoted from "Elector of Bavaria" to "King of Bavaria," which sounded much better to him.

Eugene hurried from Italy and quickly married Princess Augusta, who was quite pleased with her handsome young Viceroy. The marriage turned out to be a highly successful one, marked by lifelong love. Most of the crowned heads of Europe are their descendants, including the monarchs of Sweden, Norway, Belgium and Greece.

CHAPTER TWENTY-FIVE

NOW BONAPARTE BEGAN ALLOCATING POSITIONS of European nobility among his other family members. This was not so much to satisfy their egos as to surround France with states whose rulers would be friendly and reliable. To one still a Corsican at heart, a man's safety ultimately depended upon his family. As annoying as they could be, Bonaparte felt more comfortable with a Europe dominated by his kin.

He named Joseph King of Naples and Sicily. Despite his affliction and his troubled marriage to Hortense, Louis became King of Holland.

Temporarily at least, Lucien and Jerome were problems. Lucien refused to leave his wife, which Bonaparte made a condition to his obtaining a crown. Jerome had married an American woman Bonaparte considered unsuitable and, at first, was unable to persuade the church to grant him an annulment. Ultimately, however, Lucien got his annulment and became Prince of Canino; and Jerome, having left his American wife, became King of Westphalia.

Letizia, granted the title "Madame Mere," gathered Caroline and Elisa together to read them the list of Bonaparte's appointments. After her announcement of the two thrones to Joseph and Louis, Letizia turned to Caroline with a proud smile. "You and Murat will now be the Duke and Duchess of Berg – I believe that's quite a lovely part of Germany."

"It's evil, that's what it is!" snarled Caroline. "That bitch Hortense is to be a queen. Even frumpy Julie is to be a queen, because she's married to Joseph. And, what am I? Only a Duchess! While poor Murat, after years of loyal service to Napoleon, is to be just a Duke. It's disgusting!"

Letizia, while disappointed, was not surprised at Caroline's outburst. She turned to the less explosive Elisa.

"And you, my dear Elisa, are to be the Duchess of Tuscany, certainly an imposing title."

"And my husband?"

"I think, Elisa, that the title is yours and cannot be enjoyed by the Duchess's consort."

"Marvelous! He'll have to walk two paces behind me and bow to me when we're in public. I think he must even back away, bowing when he leaves my presence. It's absolutely marvelous!"

Letizia had reached the end of the list. "Well, there's nothing here about Pauline."

"Caroline looked up. "Why should there be? Having slept with an army of noblemen, she finally got poor Borghese to marry her. She's already a princess – which also annoys me!"

Chapter Twenty-Six

Bonaparte's popularity with the public was never greater. Nor was Josephine's.

Bonaparte threw himself into the business of governing France, dictating to his secretaries for hours at a time on every conceivable subject, from the resurfacing of roads, to the educational system, to the appointment of local officials, to the water supply in Orleans. He turned the Louvre into a museum to house not only works of French artists, but also priceless works looted from countries by the French Grande Armee. He devoted considerable time to commissioning great monuments and meeting with the architects and sculptors who were to carry out such projects. One completed project was the bronze tower in the Place Vendome. Cast entirely from captured Austrian cannons, it showed French warriors in bas relief with a statue of Bonaparte at the top.

Another project in the design phase was a gigantic monument for the top of the Champs-Élysée looking down toward the Tuilleries. At this time, the design called for an arch in the shape of a huge elephant as high as the tallest buildings in Paris and bearing depictions of Bonaparte's victories. Fortunately for Paris, the design was never carried out.

While engaging in these varied activities, Bonaparte also set to work on the design of dashing neo-classical military uniforms and an elaborate scheme of formal court etiquette.

As Emperor, Bonaparte created a new aristocracy appointed solely by him. It was different from the aristocracy of the Ancien Régime, in that it was based strictly on merit, just as the Grande Armee differed in that way from that of other nations. Dukes, Counts and Barons were created based on service to the state. They were not called the "nobility" – that sounded too much like the Ancien Régime. Instead they were called the "notables."

Despite all of his work, Bonaparte dined almost every evening alone with Josephine and often took lunch with her as well. He would also drop in on her during the day to enjoy a few moments of her calm sweetness, and he would also come to her room as she was dressing for the evening in order to supervise her attire.

The relationship of the imperial couple was never better. Josephine felt somewhat more secure since their secret religious wedding, and Bonaparte, although becoming more and more imperious with almost everyone else, seemed more loving and more playful with Josephine than ever before.

While Bonaparte was reconstructing the nation, Josephine spent considerable time at Malmaison, where she continued to increase her vast collection of exotic plants and shrubs and created a zoo with a large collection of varied animals, including llamas, a zebra, kangaroos, an orangutan and a parrot that screamed "Bonaparte! Bonaparte!" at all hours of the day and night. The animals were kept in restricted areas, rather than cages, a concept far ahead of its time.

Josephine also began a fine collection of paintings and sculpture and built a gallery at Malmaison to house and display her treasures.

Now that she was in a position to do so, Josephine also spent time providing for numerous people who had intersected with her life. She provided homes and care for her family and friends. So pronounced was her readiness to care for others, that she provided generously for Alexandre de Beauharnais' wet nurse, his illegitimate daughter and even Laure de Girardin, Beauharnais' former mistress, who had caused Josephine considerable grief in her first marriage.

But the Bonaparte family still bore Josephine ill will; and her sister-in-law, Caroline, was now the most outspoken and aggressive in that respect. One afternoon, Caroline greeted Eleonore Denuelle at the door to the Murat's Paris home. Dark eyed and slender, Eleonore was an attractive, but dull, 18 year old. She had already established a reputation for dispensing her favors liberally. Today, she was thrilled to be a guest in the home of the Emperor's sister and was anxious to hear the mysterious "proposition" at which Caroline had hinted.

After tea, a smiling Caroline led Eleonore to a little used wing of the house with a private entrance. She then showed the young girl a charmingly furnished bedroom.

"General Murat and I would like you to be our guest here, to use these quarters. Of course, you are free to come and go as you please, but we would like you to be here to see another guest, a very important guest who is very dear to me. He will drop by from time to time, sometimes without an appointment and he will be very disappointed if you are not here."

"Who is this important guest, Madame Murat?"

"I think you know."

"And what am I to do with him?"

"I think you know that too."

That night at dinner, Caroline confided in Murat what she had arranged.

"Well, Caroline, Napoleon may be pleased that you have gone to all this effort on his behalf, but why have you done it?"

"Oh God, Murat, when God gave out brains in Paris, you were in Lyon. This is not designed to get my brother fucked. It's to get Eleonore pregnant. When that happens, he'll know two things: first, that it's Josephine's fault they can't have children, and, second, that he can produce a male heir, if only he'll divorce that pretentious cow."

Chapter Twenty-Seven

During the next year, the Prussians, feeling highly vulnerable with the French army on its borders, signed a treaty of alliance with Russia and indicated their intention to join with England in another war against Bonaparte.

The Prussian King had been pushed to take this action by his Queen, a fact known to Bonaparte and one he particularly resented. Perhaps having been so spoiled by Josephine's softness and compliance, he was easily angered by strident or aggressive females – a tendency probably increased by years of dealing with his sisters.

Characteristically, Bonaparte determined to strike the Prussians quickly and decisively before the Russian forces could join them. Once again, Josephine pleaded to travel with him, and he agreed to take her along in his campaign coach as far as Mainz. They were followed by other coaches bearing Josephine's clothing and jewelry.

After an arduous ride, they arrived in Mainz, where Josephine began at once to charm the local officials. Just two days later, after a tearful farewell, Bonaparte left to take the field once again.

He moved his troops quickly and fell upon the Prussian Army at Jena, where he completely destroyed it. He then dictated extremely harsh terms to the Prussians, making it clear that he was doing so because of their meddlesome queen.

When Josephine wrote that this insult may have been unnecessary and could cause him trouble in the future, Bonaparte wrote back "It is true I detest scheming women. I am accustomed to women who are gentle, sweet and captivating, like you. It is your fault – it is you who have spoiled me for the others."

Chapter Twenty-Eight

The Prussians were crushed and were no longer a force to be considered. But the Russian army remained a formidable menace.

Bonaparte decided to move quickly again, to catch the Russian army still unprepared, to destroy it and then to negotiate a lasting peace with the Tsar that would finally leave only England as the enemy of his now vast empire.

He led his army along snow covered roads into Poland. There, two things occurred that had a significant impact on his life. First, a courier arrived from his sister Caroline with the news that Eleonore Denuelle had given birth to a healthy son. Despite the rumors that General Murat had also enjoyed the favors of his "house guest," Bonaparte was confident the child was his, the product of repeated acts of loveless and even joyless sex with the dull but attractive teenager. The news meant, of course, that he was capable of producing a male heir on someone more suitable than Eleonore Denuelle.

The second event occurred as Bonaparte led his army into the outskirts of Warsaw. Snow was falling and Bonaparte's coach was approached by the most beautiful young girl he had ever seen. She wore peasant's clothes, but her lush blonde hair, high cheekbones and ability to speak French suggested that she was not of peasant stock.

She had first found Marshall Duroc and asked to be presented to the Emperor. Stunned by her beauty and surprised at her fluent French, Duroc complied.

Now she approached the Emperor himself, who was similarly captivated. Speaking French, she said only that it was a joy to meet the man who had defeated all of the enemies of Poland. Then she disappeared into the falling snow.

"Find that girl!" Bonaparte thundered to Duroc. "The girl you brought to my coach – find her!"

"I will, sire, I will."

Two days later Duroc reported.

"Sire, the girl I brought to your coach is not a peasant at all. She is Countess Marie Walewska. She is only eighteen, but she is married to a Polish patriot, Count Walewski, and has a small son. By the way, sire, Count Walewski is seventy."

Intrigued, Bonaparte announced that he would not attend a ball given in his honor in Warsaw unless Countess Walewska was invited. The leaders of Poland, including Count Walewski, gathered to discuss the situation. They were well aware of the Emperor's reputation and what was meant by his request that the Countess attend the ball. But Poland had been dominated by Prussia, Russia and Austria, and Polish sovereignty had been destroyed. Bonaparte was Poland's only hope to regain its independence.

After vociferous protests, Marie was finally induced to go as a sacrifice for the good of her country. This was an opportunity not to be wasted. Even Count Walewski could see that and approved the decision.

Countess Walewska did attend the ball, immediately after which she received a note from Bonaparte inviting her to dine alone with him.

"At the ball I saw only you, I admired only you, I desired only you. I beg a prompt answer to calm the impatient ardor of N."

When there was no answer, "N," sent her a necklace. She refused to open the case, handing it back to the courier who brought it.

There followed a deluge of letters much like the letters he had written to Josephine at the inception of their relationship.

"Oh do not deny a measure of joy to a poor heart ready to adore you. Come to me; all your hopes will be fulfilled . . . I have brought back your country's name. I will do much more."

Finally, her husband and the other Polish patriots convinced Marie that duty to Poland required her to comply. She joined the Emperor for an intimate dinner. After the meal, which was served in his bedroom, Bonaparte began lightly to kiss her neck and shoulders and then slowly to undress her. Marie fell to the bed pretending to faint. Bonaparte surprised, but not deterred, proceeded to remove her clothes and began to practice the art of love as he had long ago been taught by Josephine. Soon, Marie, came out of her "faint" and responded readily, even enthusiastically to Bonaparte's efforts.

The rest of the night was spent together as was each subsequent night. Surprisingly, Marie became entranced with Bonaparte. Perhaps it was his power. Perhaps it was his learned skill as a lover. Perhaps it was his ardor and intensity. But she began to feel what she thought was love, as contrasted with the deep respect she felt for her husband.

When Bonaparte left with his army, leading it into East Prussia, Marie left her husband and son to move to her mother's estate. She would join the Emperor whenever and wherever he wanted her.

His summons came soon. Countess Walewska obeyed and spent many days and nights with Bonaparte, who found in her, not only youth and incomparable beauty, but also many of the qualities he admired in Josephine. She was sweet, gentle and compliant. Her primary desire, next to freeing Poland, seemed to be pleasing him in any way she could.

Surprisingly, his letters to Josephine continued to be loving and reassuring, despite the fact that he urged her repeatedly to return to Paris "to bring cheer back to the French people." To please him, she did return to the capitol, where she resumed her function as the gracious and charming Empress. Meanwhile, Bonaparte fought a vicious battle at Eylau that cost the lives of thousands of Frenchmen. He then won a tremendous victory at Friedland, resulting in the death or capture of 30,000 men.

Just before the battle of Friedland, Bonaparte received words that Hortense's small son, Napoleon Charles had died. This was, of course, a crushing blow to Hortense, but it had an additional significance for Josephine. When Bonaparte would speak of their inability to have children, he had often said that, while none of his brothers would be a worthy heir, little Napoleon Charles could be.

Now that possibility was gone, and, with Eleonore Denuelle having given birth to a healthy boy, the situation was clear – at least to Talleyrand. He stressed to Napoleon that, as Emperor of the French, he should produce a legitimate heir, and that this could be accomplished only through divorce.

Still conflicted, however, Bonaparte conceived an idea to solve the problem without a divorce. They would find a healthy young woman who would secretly bear Bonaparte's child. Meanwhile, Josephine would pretend to be pregnant. The newborn infant would be smuggled into the Palace where Josephine would "deliver" the baby, and, from the balcony, Bonaparte would proudly display his heir to the crowd below. Of course, this required the cooperation of the Emperor's physician, who adamantly refused on ethical grounds. Convinced by Talleyrand that the plan was foolhardy, Bonaparte reluctantly abandoned it. He also found a new physician.

Chapter Twenty-Nine

Bonaparte had come to realize that the key to ultimate peace in Europe was a treaty with Russia. Austria and Prussia were no longer a threat; and, if he could make peace with the Tsar, England would be isolated and forced to make peace as well. Then, at last, his Empire could be free of ever more destructive wars.

He arranged a meeting with the Tsar to hammer out just such a peace. So that neither ruler would be seen to have the weaker position, they agreed to meet on a raft in the middle of the Nieman River, dividing Russia from the rest of Europe. The raft was, of course, tented and handsomely furnished. While the Emperor and the Tsar conferred, their generals and other aides ate, drank and celebrated on the banks of the river.

Each man was fascinated with the other. Each sought to create the impression of reasonability and graciousness, rather than one of a tough bargaining. Actually, Bonaparte was sincere in taking a non-confrontational attitude. He wanted peace with Russia and was willing to be more than liberal in the terms of that peace.

The one promise he exacted from the Tsar was that Russia would adhere to Bonaparte's Continental System and shun all trade with England. The principal promise exacted by the Tsar was that Bonaparte would not create an independent Poland, which would always pose a threat to

Russia. A Poland controlled by France was acceptable. A free and independent Poland was not.

Bonaparte fully intended to keep his promise. The Tsar did not.

Chapter Thirty

"He's back, Fouché, but he's a different man." The rain pattered on the tall windows as Talleyrand limped to a chair opposite Fouché's massive desk in his Tuilleries office.

"He is certainly that. Since he's returned to Paris, he's totally full of himself, barking out orders, impatient, intolerant – imperious!"

"Well Fouché, I suppose an Emperor is supposed to be 'imperious'." Talleyrand breathed on his emerald ring and polished it on his sleeve. Then, smiling, he continued.

"The striking thing is his behavior with Josephine. He's more loving, more attentive, more playful with her than I've ever seen him."

"You're right. Talleyrand, they take their meals together, billing and cooing with each bite. They sleep together every night. It's mystifying. Just when he should be divorcing her. Even with Hortense's child gone and La Denuelle having produced a fine son – he seems more in love with his wife than ever. Not only that, even though he's brought his "Polish wife" to Paris, he rarely sees her, and he suddenly seems to have eyes only for Josephine."

"Countess Walewska is here in Paris?"

"That's what I just said. She is here and if she were to become pregnant, that would make the situation even more obvious to him, since Walewska has been with no one else. There was always a doubt about the Denuelle brat – after all, that walking erection, Joachim Murat, put his boat in Denuelle's harbor every time his wife left the house."

Talleyrand covered a yawn, "You are so poetic Fouché."

"Never mind the sarcasm. Walewska's child would clearly be Bonaparte's. It would be plain that he can produce a male heir, and just as plain that he must divorce the Empress."

"You've forgotten the words of the English Queen, Elizabeth, Fouché. 'Must is not a word one uses to monarchs.' I have spoken to him on the subject, urged him to make the decision. All he says is 'I would be giving up all that charm and love Josephine has brought to my life. She adjusts her moods, her habits, her life to mine – unselfishly. I cannot repay those years of kindness with rejection.' So Fouché, it may be clear to us. It is not so clear to him."

"Perhaps she'll take a lover one day. She's done it before, and that would do the trick with Bonaparte."

"No such luck, Fouché, Prince Frederick of Mecklenburg Strelitz is mad about her. He's young, handsome and charming; and he fawns over her like a desolate puppy. Yet she'll have no part of him. Her days of straying are over. She has no one in her life but Bonaparte, and I suspect she never will."

Two days later, Fouché encountered Josephine alone in a drawing room of the palace.

"Your majesty, may I speak to you on a subject of signal importance to the State?"

"Of course, Fouché. What is it?"

"It's the matter of divorce, your majesty. The Emperor will not speak to you about it; but France needs a male heir, and that requires your divorce. Will you not raise the subject with him, so that he can feel free to speak about it?"

Josephine turned pale. She grabbed the back of a chair to steady herself.

"Did my husband direct you to make this suggestion?"

"No, your majesty. He knows nothing of this. I spoke entirely on my own as a loyal servant of France."

"Well, Fouché, I appreciate your patriotism; but this is a personal subject I will discuss only with the Emperor. Now, if you will excuse me . . ."

That evening, after they dined together, Josephine told Bonaparte of her exchange with Fouché.

"Did you put him up to this?"

"Absolutely not, my dear."

"You think he did it on his own?"

"I'm sure of it. Fouché is like that."

"It is a grave insult, not to mention a monumental intrusion into our privacy."

Bonaparte pushed away his plate and slowly wiped his chin with a napkin. He was buying time to shape his response.

"Fouché meant no harm, my dear. He spoke in what he perceived to be the best interests of France. But you must know, my little Creole, how much I need you and that I could never be without you."

He rose and leaned close to her, stroking her face and lightly kissing her neck. They would go to Josephine's bedroom for a night of love and pleasure. But Josephine had seen Bonaparte's lack of outrage at Fouché's impertinent suggestion. It told her all she needed to know, and that knowledge was like the stab of a knife.

The days of her marriage were numbered now, and she knew it.

Chapter Thirty-One

Bonaparte was in Spain; and Josephine traveled there to join him, still retaining a glimmer of hope despite the threat of divorce that now hung over her.

After all, he had sent for her – a good sign. The Spanish situation was difficult for Bonaparte, and he needed her charm and diplomacy in dealing with the Spanish royal family. Bonaparte needed to march his army across Spain to attack Portugal, England's staunch ally. Theoretically, he would need the consent of the Spanish King. That did not seem a problem. But his plan was ultimately to depose the king and place one of his brothers on the Spanish throne.

He did not have to wait long. A massive riot broke out in Madrid, put down by French troops under Murat with great ferocity and considerable loss of life. Bonaparte advised the king that he could not survive without French protection. Otherwise, the mob would rise again and, this time, kill him, together with his family.

Without hesitation, the king abdicated in favor of the French Emperor, and the royal family was sent across the border to France, "for its safety and protection."

Now, Bonaparte and Josephine spent some time at a Spanish seaside residence. Like two children, they played on the beach, laughing, wrestling, throwing each other's clothing into the sea, and generally enjoying just being together.

Even on their return to Paris, Bonaparte was loving and attentive. They continued their playful ways, pressing friends into playing children's games at Malmaison. They were together every night, and the threat of divorce, although always present in her mind, seemed to recede somewhat.

But the news from Spain was bad. Joseph Bonaparte had been proclaimed king; but, on hearing that Marshall Junot had surrendered to the British in Portugal, Joseph had fled Madrid even before his coronation. It was clear to Bonaparte that he must personally lead a French army in Spain. No one else seemed capable of dealing effectively with the situation.

But, Bonaparte could not become bogged down in a difficult campaign in Spain only to be attacked by the vengeful Austrians and the formidable Russian army. Yes, he had the treaty of Tilsit; but could he trust the Tsar to keep it if the French army was pinned down in the Iberian Peninsula?

He arranged another meeting with the Tsar at Erfurt in Germany. Although he had said nothing about it thus far – and certainly nothing to Josephine, Bonaparte also intended to explore the possibility of marriage to the Tsar's sister. Such an alliance would more firmly commit mighty Russia to Bonaparte's cause.

In Erfurt, Bonaparte relied heavily on the diplomatic

efforts of Talleyrand, not only on the matter of the treaty of Tilsit but also on the matter of the Tsar's sister. His trust was misplaced. With the terrible situation in Spain, the English in absolute control of the sea, the rising demand in Austria and Prussia to avenge the harsh terms Bonaparte had imposed on them, Talleyrand could see nothing in France's future but war and tragedy, if she remained in the hands of Bonaparte. And, as one of the Emperor's key aides, he could see a very grim future for himself, when, as he firmly believed would occur, Bonaparte was defeated and deposed.

There was only one way to avoid that result. He must align himself secretly with the Austrians and Russians, and, as he put it to himself, he must betray Bonaparte in order to save France . . . and Talleyrand.

At Erfurt, Talleyrand spent hours with the Tsar, supposedly convincing him to remain faithful to his promises at Tilsit and even to look kindly on Bonaparte as a potential brother-in-law. In fact, Talleyrand spent those hours urging the Tsar to hold firm, to remain unyielding in his dealings with Bonaparte.

The Tsar followed Talleyrand's advice. As Bonaparte paced the room, the Tsar leaned casually against a mantel of carved malachite. "I must tell you, my friend, I have no recollection of promising to join the Continental System blocking English trade. And, in any event, such a promise would be contrary to the best interests of Russia, since my poor country is heavily dependent on British trade. I would not be fulfilling my responsibilities as Tsar should I ever make such an agreement. As to my sister, I would favor such a match, but, of course, it is entirely up to our mother, not to me."

Of course, their mother opposed any match with Bonaparte, whom she did not consider "royal" at all. To avoid further entreaties, she quickly arranged for her daughter to marry the Duke of Oldenburg.

Bonaparte left Erfurt with no material gain. Although a convention was signed dealing with minor issues, it seemed clear that the Russians would not participate in the Continental System and likely that they would join the Austrians in attacking him. And, of course, the idea of marrying the Tsar's sister was now out the window.

Worse still, public opinion in Paris was turning against him. The adventure in Spain was highly unpopular. It was considered an unnecessary war, producing thousands of casualties for what seemed an egomaniacal attempt to establish a European dynasty by placing Joseph on the Spanish throne, while giving Joseph's crown as King of Naples and Sicily to Murat, making Caroline, at last, a queen.

Yet, Bonaparte still felt he must go to Spain, personally to lead his army. He did this, but without the kind of success he had enjoyed in Europe. There were battles won and advances made, but nothing that could be called a decisive victory.

At this point, a bulletin arrived from Paris informing

him of disturbing events. The Austrians were arming again, preparing for a war in which they would join the Russians and perhaps the Prussians.

At the same time, he was confidentially advised that the two long time rivals, Talleyrand and Fouché, were seen walking arm in arm through the Tuilleries. Between the lines was a critical message – the two had formed an alliance and were almost surely plotting against him. As Bonaparte quickly grasped, all of Europe would draw that conclusion and be emboldened.

Without hesitating an hour, Bonaparte left Spain, rushing to assert himself once again in France, before the situation got out of hand.

On his return, Bonaparte summoned Talleyrand to his enormous office in the Tuilleries. He had no hard evidence of conspiracy; but there was much about Talleyrand that enraged him, not the least of which was what seemed the man's complete failure to persuade the Tsar to accept anything Bonaparte suggested. For three hours, he angrily berated his foreign minister.

Toward the end of his tirade, Bonaparte turned to the subject of the Duke of Enghein. He began to shout, "Who urged me to strike at that unfortunate young man? Who told me where he was living that I might strike at him? You – you are responsible for that infamy and for much more. You are nothing but shit in a silk stocking!"

Talleyrand stood throughout the Emperor's rant, leaning against a table to support his club foot. He made no response and his expression did not change. When Bonaparte was finally done, Talleyrand bowed, left the Palace and went directly to the Austrian Embassy, where he spoke to Count Metternich, the Austrian Ambassador.

"The time has come," Talleyrand announced cryptically. Metternich knew what he meant. Talleyrand was immediately paid one million francs. He was no longer in the service of Bonaparte, but in that of Bonaparte's enemies. More accurately, he was, and had always been, strictly in the service of Talleyrand, no matter the side to which he seemed to adhere.

And it was not only Talleyrand who had left the Imperial fold. Caroline Murat had become involved in an affair with Austria's Metternich and was plotting with him to see that Bonaparte was ultimately deposed and replaced by Murat and, of course, by Caroline herself.

Not only was Bonaparte being betrayed by Talleyrand and his sister, he was becoming increasingly unpopular with the public. The blockade of England was having an adverse effect on the French economy. And the combination of high taxes, ever growing casualty figures and the prospect of vast new conscriptions had turned much of the populace against the Emperor.

From Josephine's point of view, there was one silver lining to the dark clouds gathering overhead. As Bonaparte told Fouché, "This year is an inopportune time to shock public opinion by repudiating an Empress adored by the people. Already I am not loved. She is not only a link between me and the people, she is directly responsible for attaching a part of Paris society to me which would then desert me."

Chapter Thirty-Two

Emboldened by the French reversals in Spain, by their information that the Tsar would not stand by Bonaparte and by the assurances of Talleyrand, the Austrians not only re-armed, but invaded Bavaria, now, at least theoretically, a French ally.

Bonaparte left at once to take the field. Discovering him about to leave without warning, Josephine pleaded, in tears, to be taken along. He agreed that she might accompany him as far as Strasbourg. There, Bonaparte left her to join his new army almost half of which was comprised of recruits from Bavaria, Saxony and Poland, since the main force of the Grande Armee was still in Spain.

While Bonaparte was away, Josephine received news that Hortense had given birth to a second child, Louis Napoleon, the future Emperor Napoleon III. Josephine had a moment of hope. Here was another potential "heir" that could make divorce unnecessary. But Bonaparte did not share that view. He had been ready to consider Hortense's first child, as a potential heir, because his brother, Louis, was plainly the father and because of the widespread rumor in Paris that the real father was Bonaparte himself. "Since most people think I am the father," he had told Josephine, "I might as well make the boy my heir."

But this reasoning did not apply to the new baby. Bonaparte had serious doubts as to the child's paternity.

Hortense's marriage to Louis had never been a happy one. Louis was now afflicted with syphilis, as well as rheumatism. On his doctor's advice, he slept each night in the discarded nightshirt of a patient with running sores. He insisted that Hortense sleep with him. She obeyed, but she was utterly repulsed. Bonaparte knew that Hortense had turned to more attractive lovers, any of whom could be the father of the new born child. Also, the rumor of her sleeping with Bonaparte had long ago evaporated, so there was no reason to make this new child his heir.

Realizing that his patchwork army would not win the victories he needed, Bonaparte brought in reinforcements from Italy and France. He then led his strengthened force against the Austrians at Wagram, winning another great victory. But the cost was enormous. Fifty thousand men died in the ferocious battle.

Finding Bonaparte more preoccupied than ever before, Josephine returned to Paris discouraged and depressed. Bonaparte now ruled the French Empire from Austria. Even before Josephine left, he had installed Countess Walewska in a nearby villa. Although he saw her frequently, their relationship had cooled, perhaps because the Countess was pregnant. As Fouché had predicted, this made the matter totally clear. The paternity of Denuelle's child had been doubtful, but there could be no doubt as to the father of the child now carried by Walewska. Since she had left her husband and family in Warsaw, the beautiful Countess had slept with no one but Bonaparte.

Walewska realized sadly that Bonaparte was casting about for a royal bride, that he would divorce Josephine but would never marry her and that her child would not be the heir he had desired for so many years. She said goodbye to him at his Austrian villa. He was solicitous of her health, but obviously did not share the passion she had come to feel for him.

"Have you made plans, Marie, for yourself and the child?"

"My plans have for a long time but been centered on you, Sire. They still are."

"My sweet Marie, my future is inexorably entwined with that of France. I must place her interests about all else. I think you understand."

"I do, sadly, I do."

"What I recommend Marie, is that you return to your husband. He is a brave patriot and a splendid man. We have spoken. He is not only willing, but anxious to have you back, he will make the child his and give it his name."

"Then you have arranged my future for me."

"I have my dearest. Someone had to."

Chapter Thirty-Three

After years of indecision and procrastination, Bonaparte had finally decided to act on the divorce. He returned to France and sent a message directing Josephine to meet him at Fontainebleau. Given his decision, Bonaparte sought to avoid resuming his loving relationship with Josephine. He tried to find reasons to be angry with her, but he could not. He tried everything he could to push her away. When she arrived at Fontainebleau, he was already present and greeted her coldly. When shown to her quarters, she learned that the door between their bedrooms had been sealed.

No longer did Bonaparte dine with her. Instead, he pointedly dined with his sister, Pauline, and her guests, a sight Josephine could see as she passed to and from her own apartment.

When he encountered Josephine, he was surly and cold, bringing her frequently to tears. He simply could not deal with the situation otherwise. If he tried tenderness, he knew he would relent. So he cloaked his guilt and sadness with feigned anger.

Once again he asked Hortense to tell her mother of his need for a divorce. As before, she refused. Nor did he have greater success with Eugene. He realized finally that he must tell her himself. There was no one else.

Bonaparte began to dine with Josephine once more, planning to tell her of his decision during a meal. Instead, they sat in silence pushing their food around, neither eating.

Finally, on one such evening, Bonaparte rose from the table asking Josephine to join him in the next room. Once there he told her of his decision.

Outside the closed doors loud screams could be heard. When an aide was finally asked by Bonaparte to enter, Josephine was stretched out on the floor hysterically weeping.

Bonaparte and the aide carried her to her apartment. Now he was also in tears. He mumbled to the aide something about his duty to France and his heart being broken. Then he sent for Hortense.

When Hortense arrived, Bonaparte was still dabbing at his eyes with his handkerchief. He turned to her and announced stubbornly, "Nothing will make me go back on it, neither tears nor entreaties."

Hortense put her hand on his arm soothingly. "You are the master, Sire. No one will oppose you. Do not be surprised at my mother's tears. It would surely be more surprising if, after a union of thirteen years, she did not shed them. She will submit, and we will all go away, taking the memory of your kindness with us."

Bonaparte, overwhelmed by self-pity, cried out, "What! You are all going to leave me? You are going to desert me? You don't care for me any more?"

With her mother's poise and sweetness, Hortense tried to calm him.

"You must understand. I owe myself to my mother. We cannot live with you or even near you any longer. It is a sacrifice we have to make, and we will make it."

Soon Eugene arrived, having heard of what had occurred. Immediately, Bonaparte returned to his theme of self-pity.

"Eugene, I cannot bear the thought of the three of us being forever apart. I simply cannot! Perhaps I should suspend the divorce, stay with all of you. Nothing is irrevocable. I am, after all the Emperor."

"Sire, surely you must see it is too late. What was in your mind has now been spoken – to our mother and to us. It cannot be unspoken, and, given those words, our mother could not continue to live with you without going mad."

Bonaparte shook his head as if to make the problem disappear.

"Look, Eugene, I've caused your mother great sorrow and you have done me loyal service for years. I will make you King of Italy."

Eugene smiled. "Sire, I appreciate your confidence and your offer. But, I could never accept something that appeared to be in repayment for my mother's tears, and the Kingdom of Italy surely would be just that. I suggest, Sire, that you leave us now, so that we may comfort our mother."

CHAPTER THIRTY-FOUR

THE OFFICIAL DIVORCE CEREMONY was a state occasion. The entire court, resplendent in all of their finery, decorations and jewelry was present by imperial command.

Josephine made a dramatic entrance dressed in a plain white muslin gown and walking with grace and composure. She was escorted by Hortense and a pale Eugene, shaking with emotion.

When the murmur of the audience had subsided, Bonaparte rose. He too was pale and trembling. After formally announcing the divorce, he looked around the room, paused and then spoke to the rapt audience in a low voice, shaking with emotion.

"God alone knows what this resolve has cost my heart. I have found courage for it only in the conviction that it serves the best interests of France. I have only gratitude to express for the devotion and tenderness of my well-beloved wife. She has adorned thirteen years of my life; the memory thereof will remain forever engraved upon my heart."

He stood for another moment, tears streaming down his cheeks. Then he resumed his seat.

Now, Josephine rose to speak. She looked down at her prepared notes, rather than at the audience.

"With the permission of my dear and august husband,

I proudly offer him the greatest proof of attachment and devotion ever given a husband on this earth and . . ."

At this point her voice broke, and tears came. Twice, she tried to resume, but she could not. Finally, she handed her speech to an aide, who read it for her, while she sat quietly weeping.

Bonaparte and Josephine then signed the official document of divorce. When this was done, Bonaparte surprised the audience by kissing her and leading her by the hand to her apartment.

Later that night, after the throng had left, Josephine came to his bedroom. She fell on the bed, put her arms around Bonaparte's neck and covered him with tender kisses. Both began to weep, and they lay there just holding each other, well into the night.

Chapter Thirty-Five

THE NEXT DAY, Josephine left for Malmaison, accompanied by Hortense, Eugene and trunks full of clothing, jewelry and other possessions. Knowing that she loved it and torn by feelings of guilt, Bonaparte gave her the house and grounds. In addition, he provided the Élysée Palace as her Paris residence, plus the stupendous allowance of three million francs per year. In addition, all of her substantial debts were paid, and she was to retain the title of Empress.

Bonaparte felt that, at Malmaison, Josephine would, at least be soothed by the comfortable rooms she had decorated and by her garden, her hothouse full of exotic plants and her small, but unique zoo.

Malmaison helped; but that first day found Josephine inconsolable. Bonaparte too was miserable. Locking himself in his library in the Grand Trianon, he brooded about what he had done.

The next day, he drove in the rain to Malmaison. He and Josephine walked hand in hand along the wet garden pathway talking about the strange turn their lives had taken.

It rained every day that week, and, ever day, Bonaparte made the pilgrimage to Malmaison, to walk and talk with Josephine, but essentially just to be near her. So strong were his feelings for her that, after four days, he suggested that, despite their divorce, they should find some discreet place, where, at least most of the time, they could quietly live together.

Josephine, her heart aching, told him it was not a good idea, that it would make the situation even more unbearable.

Well," he said, putting his arm around her, "maybe after the first year."

Chapter Thirty-Six

DESPITE HIS FEELINGS FOR JOSEPHINE, Bonaparte continued to pursue the idea of a dynastic marriage. He had suggested to the Tsar the possibility of a match with still another of the Tsar's sisters, this one only a teenager. The Tsar provided only equivocal answers, and Bonaparte began to sense that, ultimately, he would receive an outright rejection, and that it would make him the laughing stock of Europe.

To avoid this embarrassment, he took swift and decisive action. He called Eugene to his palace library. "You, my son, are the only one I can trust with this highly sensitive mission and, given the identity of your mother, you will give added credibility to my suit."

Within an hour, Eugene was in the lavishly decorated office of the Austrian Ambassador, who had donned his full dress uniform for the sudden meeting with the Emperor's adopted son.

"Will you have a coffee, Monsieur Beauharnais – or I should more appropriately say your highness."

"No thank you, your excellency. I will only be a few minutes, and 'Monsieur Beauharnais' is perfectly all right.

"Ah . . . I'm sorry you are pressed for time. I ordered some of our splendid Viennese pastries." He gestured toward an ornate silver platter piled with delicate cakes of various shapes and designs.

"That is indeed a shame, your excellency, but perhaps some other time. Today, my mission is simple and straightforward. The Emperor wishes the hand in marriage of your Princess Marie Louise."

The Ambassador rose, smiling.

"Ah, Beauharnais, that is an extraordinary and gratifying suggestion. I will, of course, pass it on to her father in Vienna and will provide the Emperor with a prompt and, I am sure, favorable response."

Now, Eugene rose. "I don't think I have been entirely clear, your excellency. The Emperor insists that his proposal be accepted today and that the marriage contract be signed tomorrow. Otherwise, the proposal will be withdrawn, and the Emperor will move in another direction entirely."

"But, monsieur, that is impossible! The fastest courier would take days to reach Vienna and days to return. The decision is one of huge importance to our two nations and to the future life of the Princess. It cannot be made in a matter of hours."

"The Emperor is convinced that you as the accredited representative of Austria have the power and authority to make this decision in behalf of your great nation."

The ambassador pulled a handkerchief from his sleeve and mopped his brow.

"But monsieur, what you ask – what the Emperor asks – is unprecedented. It is simply not possible. It . . . "

But Eugene interrupted him, speaking in a voice of icy calm.

"Well then, your excellency, if you will not exercise your manifest authority in this matter, I need not tarry here – the Emperor's proposal is revoked. He will, of course, be extremely displeased – indeed insulted. And I suspect that your own masters in Vienna will seriously regret this outcome. Good day, sir." He turned to leave.

"No wait, Beauharnais!" cried the Ambassador, moving from behind his desk and placing a hand on Eugene's arm, as if to stay him, "I am certainly not rejecting the Emperor's proposal – no, far from it – I rejoice at receiving it. I rejoice! Can you allow me just a few minutes to confer with my colleagues? Please sit down. Sit, sit! Have a pastry!"

In twenty minutes, the Ambassador returned. Rising to his full height, he spoke in a stentorian tone. "On behalf of the nation of Austria, the Princess Marie Louise and her father, the ruler of that great nation, the esteemed request of the Emperor of the French for the hand of the princess in marriage, is hereby accepted."

On hearing Eugene's report, Bonaparte laughed, then swiftly moved to phase two of his plan. He immediately sent two couriers speeding to Russia. One carried a personal message to the Tsar telling him that the Emperor had decided against marriage to his sister. The second courier carried a formal announcement of the Emperor's impending marriage to Princess Marie Louise of Austria.

Bonaparte had not acted a moment too soon. As his couriers raced across the Russian plain, they passed a Russian courier speeding westward bearing a message from the Tsar. That message arrived three days later. It announced that the Tsar regretfully declined to give his sister to the Emperor in marriage.

By then, of course, the entire world – at least the entire world that counted to Bonaparte – knew that the Emperor of the French was marrying the Austrian princess. Try as he might, the Tsar was unable to convince anyone that his message of rejection, coming days after the official engagement of Bonaparte to Marie Louise, was anything but sour grapes.

Chapter Thirty-Seven

In Vienna, the court was in a celebratory mood. The threat of the French "ogre" would now be diminished. Prince Metternich, the Austrian Foreign Minister, praised his Ambassador in Paris for a courageous and wise decision made under unimaginable pressure. But what he said after that praise belied the spirit of general merriment.

"From now on, we must move with great care. We must avoid any military confrontation with Bonaparte. We must cajole and flatter him – until the day of deliverance."

Bonaparte sent Marshal Berthier to Vienna to stand in for him at the proxy marriage of the Princess and the Emperor. To satisfy the concerns in Vienna about the validity of his divorce, Bonaparte induced the Parisian officials to grant him an annulment, on the grounds that the clerk who performed his marriage was unauthorized and that Bonaparte had been "coerced" by Josephine. There was considerable laughter in Paris and Vienna over the latter ground, but what doubts had existed were satisfied or at least silenced. Of course, nothing was said about the secret religious ceremony on the eve of Bonaparte's coronation.

Bonaparte wrote Josephine advising her to stay at the Élysée Palace, so that he could see her more often, since, as she must know, he still loved her. Despite this, he became so immersed in the plans for his formal wedding in Paris that he had little time for Josephine or, for the most part, anyone or anything else.

Three weeks after the proxy wedding, Marie Louise was on her way by coach to the Château de Compiègne, where Louis XVI had been married to her great aunt, Marie Antoinette, and where she would be formally married to the Emperor of the French.

As usual, Bonaparte decided on direct action. This marriage had a purpose and he would fulfill that purpose – now! Having sent Marie Louise a series of love letters that awaited her at every stop of her journey, he intercepted her on the road to Compiègne. As the steps of her coach were lowered, the Princess's aide cried out "The Emperor" kneeling, as best he could inside the coach. To the surprise of the Princess, Bonaparte leapt into the coach with her, directing the aide to leave and the driver to proceed at once to Compiègne.

The light was dim, but Bonaparte could see that she was much like the portraits he had been shown. She was blonde, fair, pleasant looking, perhaps a bit on the heavy side (compared to Josephine), but undoubtedly a healthy young woman, likely to bear healthy children. Slyly, he began stroking her leg, moving ever closer to her inner thigh, as the coach flew down the muddy road to Compiègne.

At the chateau, royal families from all over the continent were waiting with champagne and flowers to greet the new princess. Descending with her from the coach, Bonaparte took her arm and, to the consternation of the royal throng, he led her straight past them, upstairs to her bedroom.

Then, he called for Uncle Fesch and spoke to him quietly outside the hearing of the Princess.

"Uncle, am I married to this girl or not?"

"Civilly you are married to her. In the eyes of the Church, however, you are not yet married."

"Well," he said, shooing the Cardinal from the room, "I am a civil man."

He turned to Marie Louise and gave her an order in his most imperious tone, "Undress and get into bed. I will join you immediately." Trained to obedience, the Princess did as she was commanded. Removing her clothes, she slipped into the vast bed. Without hesitating, the Emperor removed all of his clothing except his silk shirt. Then he moved into the bed next to her.

He began a feather-like stroking of her inner thighs coming teasingly ever closer to her loins. She began almost involuntarily to raise her hips to meet the delicate strokes that were already sending spears of pleasure through her surprised young body.

As he bent to kiss her erect pink nipples, she whispered, "Sire, are we married?"

"Married, my dear? Of course we are."

At that, she threw her arms around him and kissed him as passionately as she knew how.

When Bonaparte had finished demonstrating all the extraordinary things he had learned so long ago from

Josephine, he withdrew from her utterly spent and rolled onto his side, still facing her.

"So, my little rabbit, what do you think of married life?"

Marie Louise rose on one elbow looking down at him with a strange expression.

"Do it again, Sire. Oh, do it again."

CHAPTER THIRTY-EIGHT

FRANCE HAD A NEW EMPRESS, but the sentimental favorite with the court, the army and the public was still Josephine. Everyone remembered her charm, her poise, her ability to speak to the point, yet always with tact, grace and sweetness.

Marie Louise, by contrast, seemed lumpish, both physically and socially. She appeared unable to carry on an intelligent conversation and her few attempts at addressing a gathering were disastrous. Her relationship with the Bonaparte family was no better than Josephine's had been, but for a totally different reason. Marie Louise dismissed Bonaparte's hostile sisters as "low born Corsican riffraff."

But, Marie Louise had one trump card. She was pregnant. Even so, she was intensely jealous of Josephine. One day when Bonaparte and his new young wife were out driving near Malmaison, he suggested that she might like to see the house, explaining that he knew Josephine was away in Paris. After a moment of silence, Marie Louise began sobbing uncontrollably.

Josephine, always confident in her ability to win over anyone with her charm and sweetness, asked Bonaparte to arrange for her to meet Marie Louise. "I cannot," he replied. "She thinks you are very old. If she ever sees you, she would ask me to send you away permanently, and I would have to do it."

Bonaparte asked that Josephine not remain at Malmaison at this critical time. Making sure she understood that he still cared for her deeply, he asked that, given Marie Louise's jealous disposition, Josephine should winter in Italy, where he would make for her the most comfortable arrangements imaginable.

Josephine complied with his wishes. She spent the next year traveling in Italy and Switzerland before returning to Malmaison.

The house there remained untouched. Bonaparte's things, which he had never removed, remained just as they had been. Josephine received a flattering proposal of marriage from Prince Frederick Louis of Mecklenburg-Strelitz, who had adored her for years. She rejected his proposal. There was only one man in her life, although he was now married to someone else.

Chapter Thirty-Nine

FINALLY, IT WAS TIME for Marie Louise to give birth. Despite her apparent health and strength, the birth turned out to be difficult and dangerous. The physician advised Bonaparte that it was unlikely they could save both the mother and the child and that the Emperor must make a choice.

Bonaparte made a lightning-like calculation. If Marie Louise died, the Austrian connection would wither, despite the birth of a child. If the child died, Marie Louise and he would have the sympathy of all Europe, the Austrian connection would remain strong and she could have other children.

"Save the mother!" he said to the physician, who prepared to follow that instruction. As the baby was taken from Marie Louise, it appeared to be stillborn. It was a boy, but he was silent and immobile, his color a sickly blue. The nurse gently set the infant on a table and turned away in tears. The physician refused to give up. He gave the infant a hearty smack on the bottom. Almost immediately the boy started crying and breathing. Slowly, he took on a rosy hue. The male heir had been born.

There was great rejoicing in Paris over the birth of the child. A 21 gun salute had been planned if the child was a girl, with 100 guns for a boy. When the cannon fire began, Parisians rushed to their windows to count. When the 22nd gun was fired, a huge roar could be heard throughout the city, and the people poured into the streets dancing and shouting.

At last France had the male heir for whom the Emperor had yearned. He was to be called the "King of Rome."

Chapter Forty

After months of traveling, Josephine returned to Malmaison. In Milan, she had enjoyed spending time with her four grandchildren by Eugene and Augusta; and, at Malmaison, she frequently saw Louis Napoleon, Hortense's son, an extremely bright child, who, as Napoleon III, would look back with great fondness to times spent with his loving grandmother at Malmaison. He recalled its strange and beautiful plants and its remarkable zoo. It was a magic place for a young boy.

But, the child Josephine desperately wanted to meet was Napoleon's son, the King of Rome. She felt that a child of Bonaparte's was a part of her life and someone she must know and love. Over and over again she pleaded with him to allow the boy to visit Malmaison. Finally, with all the secrecy of a surprise military raid, he arranged for a clandestine meeting between the two, as the child's governess was walking him in a nearby wood. As the governess had been instructed, she left Josephine and the boy alone, discreetly sitting on a bench some distance away, as the tiny child and the dowager Empress played games, ran races and hugged each other for almost an hour. When the time came to part, Josephine threw her arm around the boy, close to tears.

She begged Bonaparte for another visit; but Marie Louise had discovered the meeting in the wood and, enraged, had forbidden any repetition.

In this period Josephine entertained many friends and visiting dignitaries at Malmaison, which had become something between an informal court and a lively salon. As always, she charmed her guests with her wit and grace and entranced them with exotic fruit from her garden and the extraordinary dishes of her superb Italian chef. Still the Empress, she had filled the house with professional staff ready to provide for a guest's every wish, and, when she went for a drive, she was accompanied by fourteen cuirassiers on prancing mounts, their silver helmets and breastplates flashing in the sum.

But the pleasant life at Malmaison was like a fantastic island in a sea of discontent. The Emperor's court, without Josephine to provide gaiety and charm, had become a stiff and joyless place. The Emperor himself had become more irritable and short tempered. Without Josephine, he was simply not the same man. Marie Louise was hardly a help.

Even the public as a whole tended to be depressed and unsatisfied. The war in Spain, still perceived as unnecessary, cost more and more French lives every month, the army seemed no closer to success, and the Emperor seemed unable or unwilling to take personal command.

The nation was also plagued by inflation, high taxes and increasing unemployment. The Emperor seemed unconcerned as the price of bread and other essentials exceeded what the general public could afford. The nation was facing a financial crisis, and the Emperor's popularity was at the lowest point since his coronation.

Talleyrand and Fouché began to give each other knowing looks. The signs were there. They resolved to insure that, when the upheaval came, they would be with the victors, not the vanquished.

Chapter Forty-One

As the domestic situation worsened, the Emperor's foreign problems grew as well. Bonaparte received word that, despite his marriage to Marie Louise, the Austrians were re-arming. He knew they weren't preparing to fight the Russians or the Prussians. If they were raising another army, it had to be to fight the French.

And the Tsar seemed set on a collision course with France. He had reopened Russian trade with England, violating his promise at Tilsit and ruining Bonaparte's scheme to crush England economically. He seemed even readier than the Austrians to take on the French Grande Armee and certainly more capable of doing so.

Although much of his army was still pinned down in Spain, Bonaparte determined to attack Russia with massive and overwhelming force. He raised an army of 675,000 men, many of whom were drawn from vassal states, such as Germany, Holland, Italy and Poland. At the time, it was the largest army that had ever been assembled.

Before launching his attack on Russia, Bonaparte traveled to Dresden with Marie Louise to meet with the Austrians, hoping to persuade them to remain neutral in the coming fight. He received the assurances he sought, but Bonaparte was a realist. He grasped that the Austrians resented the terms he had imposed upon them in the past and that Prince Metternich was by no means his friend. He knew that despite the new Austrian promises, and even his Austrian marriage, if his attack on Russia went badly, he could not count on Austrian support or even Austrian neutrality.

Of course, with his massive army and his own military skill, he did not expect things to go badly. He wrote cheerful, affectionate letters to both Marie Louise and Josephine. He anticipated a great victory, a final conquest of mother Russia.

With that as his goal, the Emperor marched his vast army across Eastern Europe and into Russia. The Tsar, while somewhat unreliable in performing treaty obligations, was no fool. Neither was General Kutuzov, who commanded the Russian army. They were aware that they lacked sufficient manpower to defend Russia against Bonaparte's huge force. So they adopted a unique strategy. They knew that Bonaparte did not believe in cumbersome supply trains following his fighting men into foreign lands, that, instead, the French army lived off the land, taking the food and supplies it needed in the countries it invaded. This accomplished two goals. It allowed the Grande Armee to travel vast distances without concern for its lines of supply, and it punished those who resisted by forcing them to pay for their own occupation.

To defeat this strategy, the Tsar decreed that all the crops and even the buildings in the path of the French invasion be burned and that all livestock be destroyed or moved away before the French arrived. The invaders must find nothing to eat, no shelter, nothing to aid them in any way.

As Bonaparte's army moved deeper and deeper into Russia, with forced marches and little rest, hunger and fatigue took a serious toll. Every week, many hundreds of his troops deserted, particularly those from vassal states, but even many of the French.

The Russians tended to avoid any pitched battle, just skirmishing, raiding and retreating, deeper and deeper into Russian territory. Finally, recognizing that the French were seriously weakened, Kutuzov determined to weaken them further with a costly fight, even if it was costly for Russia as well. Surprising Bonaparte, the Russians stood and fought at Borodino. The losses on both sides were grievous. At the end of the day the Russians left the field to the French. But was this a victory? Bonaparte knew better. Borodino had bled his already staggering army severely. Now he had to get his depleted and starving forces into Moscow before winter set in. If he could not, they were done for.

With more forced marches, Bonaparte accomplished that goal. As his weary troops entered Moscow, it was silent and deserted. Well, Bonaparte thought, I didn't expect the streets to be lined with cheering citizens, and at least there will be housing for us during the ferocious Russian winter.

That evening, however, resting in his new Moscow headquarters, Bonaparte suddenly heard numerous loud explosions. They seemed to be coming, one after the other, from all around him. The Russians had set off powerful incendiary bombs in every section of the city. In half an hour all of Moscow was hopelessly ablaze.

With neither shelter nor food available in the Russian capitol, Bonaparte was left with no choice. He gave the order to retreat. Somehow, he must bring what was left of his depleted army out of this Russian hell, across Eastern Europe and all the way back to France.

And so, the weary, starving units of the once proud Grande Armee started the endless trek across Russia, as the snow began to fall and the cruel Russian winter began.

There was little or no food to be found, no shelter, little medicine and no replacements for their worn-through boots. Slowly, one by one, the horses began to die, and the men lived on their meat. Soon that was gone too; and there was nothing except a few straggly plants still rising above the snow. Men died by the thousands every day, and not all from hunger.

As the military units broke apart into scattered groups and individuals trying, against staggering odds to reach the border, the Cossacks, fierce cavalrymen accustomed to the Russian winter, began a series of deadly harassing attacks, usually by day, but sometimes at night, so that even sleep was difficult.

By mid-November, Bonaparte's army, so massive when it proudly crossed the Russian border, was reduced to a small fraction of its original size. Bonaparte had lost over half a million men, captured, deserted or, in most cases, dead. More were being lost each day.

Bonaparte decided it was time to leave. Bundled in the back of a swift horse drawn sleigh, he abandoned what was left of his army and raced over the frozen wastes back to Paris. He believed that, once there, a personal display on his part would offset the terrible news that would, sooner or later, find its way from Russia to the French capitol.

Upon his arrival in Paris, Bonaparte drove almost immediately to Malmaison to see Josephine, who had been terrified for him, as well as for Eugene. Her son had taken over command of what was left of the troops after Murat, placed in charge by Bonaparte, left the retreating force, pleading illness. Bonaparte calmed her as best he could, assuring her that Eugene would be safe. She clung to him affectionately, as if, somehow, he had returned to her. But his problem was with the public, not Josephine.

At first, his plan seemed to be working. Even though Parisians sensed that the news was bad, the fact that the Emperor had returned and was conducting himself in a normal fashion seemed to allay the public's concern – at least for the moment.

But this reprise could not continue. Despite Bonaparte's attempt to divert the citizens with quickly arranged grand balls and fetes, the horrendous news that the Grande Armee had been utterly destroyed gradually filtered into the streets, homes and shops throughout the nation. Almost everyone had a family member or friend who had died in the disastrous campaign.

The public's initial acceptance now turned to bitter resentment. To the public, the Emperor was now a man who had abandoned his army and returned to dances and merriment, while his loyal troops died in the snow.

The impact on the rest of Europe was also dramatic. Bonaparte was no longer considered invincible or even that formidable. All the resentment that had been brewing in countries like Prussia and Austria, upon whom Bonaparte had imposed harsh and humiliating terms, was now boiling over. The King of Prussia concluded an alliance with the Tsar. England and Spain were already fighting, and Austria was ready to join in the fray. Prince Metternich's "day of deliverance" was finally at hand.

Chapter Forty-Two

With an outward show of optimism, Bonaparte quickly mobilized another large force and took the field once more. Bands playing and flags flying, one more army moved out of Paris, cheered by fewer Parisians in the streets than ever before.

Bonaparte knew he must fight the Russians, although any thoughts of invading Russia were now gone forever. He was unsure about the Prussians, and, given Marie Louise and their son, he still hoped that the Austrians might remain neutral.

After a few inconclusive battles, Bonaparte asked the Tsar for an armistice. They agreed to mediation by the Austrians, a process Bonaparte believed would be to his advantage. He was wrong. The mediator's terms were for France to return to its much smaller pre-Bonaparte borders, a proposal surprising to Bonaparte, coming as it did from his own father-in-law. He rejected it out of hand and returned at once to Paris. It was a serious mistake.

Given Bonaparte's rejection of the peace terms and his perceived weakness, the Austrians joined the coalition of the Russians and Prussians. With renewed war a certainty, even Bonaparte's marshals were now unsure of the caliber of his leadership or even his will to lead.

Nevertheless, he took the field again, having conscripted an even larger, but less experienced army, a measure enormously unpopular.

Josephine was terrified both for Bonaparte and for Eugene, who had survived the retreat from Moscow and remained in command of the French forces in the East, where the fighting would surely occur.

Her anxiety was somewhat eased by the arrival of Hortense's two sons at Malmaison and by the frequent visits of Countess Walewska with Bonaparte's son Alexandre. Paris buzzed with gossip at the friendship between the two women, but Josephine continued to consider Bonaparte the most important part of her life and any connection with him – even if it was Walewska and her son – was dear to her.

Soon Josephine heard the bad news that Bonaparte had been defeated by the coalition armies at the battle of Leipzig. Once again, his luck seemed to have deserted him. She wrote him, pouring her feelings into the page.

"Although I may no longer share in your joys, your grief will always be mine too. I can no more resist telling you of this than I could cease to love you with all my heart."

Bonaparte raced back to Paris in a desperate attempt to raise still more men and money. This was now an extremely difficult task. The French were well aware that he had lost almost a million men in slightly more than a year. The concept of still more conscription, still more deaths, created public outrage.

Alone in his library, Bonaparte contemplated his situation. It seemed that, ever since he had parted from Josephine, destiny's touch had left him. Everything had gone wrong since then. Everything!

Soon, he had to face not only the oncoming force of the European coalition, but also the sting of betrayal by his vassal states and, worse, by his friends and family. When the King of Wurttemburg abandoned him, it was not unexpected. But, when his sister, Elisa, negotiated with his enemies seeking to regain her territories as Grand Duchess of Tuscany, it was a severe blow. Far worse, however, were his sister Caroline and her husband, Marshall Murat. Having abandoned his command on the Eastern front to Eugene, Murat now signed a treaty with the Austrians, agreeing to support the coalition against Bonaparte in exchange for a guarantee of the throne of Naples for himself. Bonaparte's sister, Caroline, had supported her husband in this act of breathtaking betrayal.

Through it all, Eugene remained steadfast. While all the others around him were seeking, in any way possible, to save their own skins, Eugene flatly rejected the offer of his father-in-law, the King of Bavaria, to become King of Italy if he would only forsake Bonaparte and join the coalition.

Unlike Caroline, Murat, Elisa and so many others, Eugene was incapable of such betrayal. In this regard, he was his mother's son, imbued with her sense of loyalty. As he wrote to her, "The Emperor's star pales, but that is a further reason to remain faithful to him."

Josephine read Eugene's letter standing in the garden at Malmaison. She felt a fierce pride at her son's principled stand. She wished there was some way he could help Bonaparte; but she feared he was beyond the help of anyone.

Chapter Forty-Three

By March, the coalition forces had crossed the Rhine. Soon, Parisians could hear the distant sound of cannon fire. Refugees from east of the capital began to clog the roads and there were rumors of bands of wild Cossacks killing and raping as they rode through French villages.

Josephine left Malmaison for Chateau de Navarre, a provincial house given her by Bonaparte many years before. Not knowing what lay in the future, she had sewn her diamonds in the hems of her petticoats. Hortense and the children were to follow her to Navarre.

As soon as Josephine left, her staff began packing to leave as well. Some had already replaced the tricolor cockades they had worn in their hats and buttonholes for years, as symbols of the revolution, with the white cockades of the Bourbon monarchy.

Marie Louise and her son left the capitol heading south as directed by Joseph Bonaparte. He urged her to go to her father and appeal to him to deal generously with the family. She was not ready to do that, hoping still to join Bonaparte and to share whatever might be his fate.

While so many were fleeing Paris, Talleyrand stayed. He wanted to be on hand to play a significant role in what he saw as a likely restoration of Bourbon rule. He smiled as he supervised the rehanging of a portrait of Louis XVIII in the foyer of his palatial home.

From the hills of Montmartre, Joseph Bonaparte watched the fighting on the outskirts of the city. Discouraged by what he saw, he authorized Marshall Marmont to surrender the city and left for Blois to join the Bonaparte family.

Finally, on April 1st, the coalition troops marched in triumph down the Champs-Élysées. The streets of the capitol were deserted. Parisians had no idea what to expect, but were stunned at the sight of Russians, Austrians and Prussians flooding the boulevards of their capitol.

That same evening, the Tsar arrived in Paris. He occupied Talleyrand's lavish mansion, having been falsely warned by Talleyrand that all the palaces were probably mined.

At Talleyrand's home the leaders of the coalition forces met to decide on the future government of France. There was doubt among them, particularly on the part of the Tsar, that the French would accept the return of the aging, obese Louis XVIII, now in exile in England. But the ever ready Talleyrand assured the group that France would embrace a Bourbon restoration, so long as it was constitutional in form.

Ultimately that was the decision, and a provisional government was set up to rule until Louis XVIII could return from England to take the throne. Who would head the provisional government? There seemed only one logical choice – It was, of course, Talleyrand, the ultimate survivor.

Meanwhile, Bonaparte had been fighting desperate battles against overwhelming odds, trying to make his way into the capitol to defend those parts of the city not yet occupied. At Fontainebleau, he called his marshals together to decide on their next move. As the meeting began, a courier arrived from the capitol. "Sire, Paris has surrendered."

"Nonsense! Who would surrender the capitol?"

"It was surrendered by General Marmont on the orders of Joseph Bonaparte."

Bonaparte flew into a rage. "This is treachery! This cannot be! My own brother, my God!"

Calmed after a moment, he reached for a map. Unrolling it, he began pointing to areas within a few days march.

"We have troops here, here and *here*" he said, stabbing at the map with his finger. "Within four days I can have them concentrated at Fontainebleau – probably fifty thousand men. We can call in reinforcements from all the occupied territories. We have at least 100,000 more men out there. With our 50,0000, we'll fight a delaying action until the reinforcements arrive. Paris is not France, gentlemen! The enemy may hold the capitol, but we will hold the rest of the country and, eventually, we will drive them out!"

He resumed his seat, slumping as if exhausted. One by one, his marshals rose, telling him in no uncertain terms that the situation was hopeless.

"There is only one solution, Sire. Remember the Duke of Enghein. Believe me, your enemies do. If you want to save yourself, to avoid prison or worse, you must abdicate."

"I would only abdicate in favor of my son, the King of Rome. My father-in-law will agree, I'm sure."

Now Bonaparte's old friend, Coulaincourt, rose. "That will not work, Sire. They will never accept it. Sadly, your trust in your father-in-law is misplaced. He is your worst enemy. Your abdication must be unconditional. Only in that way will you be spared."

Finally, speaking in a tired voice, without rising, Bonaparte agreed. He was handed a document of abdication that had already been prepared. Shaking his head, as if in a daze, he signed it. With a stroke of the pen, an era had ended. Napoleon Bonaparte was no longer Emperor of the French.

At the urging of the Tsar, the coalition agreed that Bonaparte would be made ruler of the Island of Elba off the coast of Italy and that he would be granted a generous allowance.

The morning fog still clung to the ground, as an elite regiment of the Imperial Guard assembled in the palace courtyard to hear Bonaparte's farewell. He emerged from the palace, a small man in an unadorned great coat. Removing the familiar black hat, he stepped forward to address them.

"Men of the Guard. You have served France and your Emperor with great courage and skill. I will never forget you."

Bonaparte moved to the tall, grizzled sergeant who held the regimental colors.

"If I could, I would kiss every one of you. Let this be our farewell kiss."

With this, he took the flag in his hand and tenderly kissed it. Then, quickly, he turned and was gone.

At Navarre, Josephine heard of Bonaparte's abdication, of his relegation to Elba and that Talleyrand would head the provisional government. Not realizing that Talleyrand's betrayal had been a principal cause of Bonaparte's downfall, she wrote to him seeking his advice and help. Then she wrote to Eugene, asking him to join her and Hortense, so that their fate would be shared. She had no idea what that fate might be.

Talleyrand, always thinking ahead, realized that Josephine was loved and admired by the public and that she could be very important to the new Bourbon government in which he expected to play an important role. He responded to her letter, reassuring her of her safety and that of her family and promising large annuities for herself and Hortense.

Now, Louis XVIII returned to France. Parisians were shocked at his appearance. After many years of absence he had grown monstrously fat and so severely afflicted with gout that he had to be supported by two aides whenever he chose to move on foot, which was not often.

While there was no uprising against him, the King was hardly popular. What was popular was the concept of peace – peace at last, after years of fighting, constant conscription, a million dead and a generation of young men virtually wiped out.

Still, while a few gentlemen with royalist inclinations or political ambitions wore the Bourbon lily, the bulk of the people were decidedly cool about this fat old man who would be their King.

Advised by Talleyrand, the Tsar and Metternich grasped the inherent instability of the situation. Meeting with them, Talleyrand rose, leaning on a desk to support his crippled leg.

"Your majesty – your excellency," he said nodding to the two men and bowing obsequiously, "I have a solution."

"What is it Monsieur President?"

Talleyrand smiled slyly. "The solution is not an 'it.' It is a woman – the dowager Empress Josephine. She is trusted and beloved by the people. If she appears to support the restoration, even if she will only return to the capitol and proceed to lead her prior life, it will be a critical signal to the public that the new regime is acceptable."

The Tsar and Prince Metternich nodded to each other in agreement. That day, each sent word to Josephine assuring her safety and that of her family and urging her to return to Malmaison as soon as would be convenient. The Tsar even sent a troop of Cossacks to guard her both at Navarre and en route to Malmaison.

Meanwhile, the Tsar bravely walked the streets of Paris virtually unattended. He quickly won the admiration of the Parisians, who were impressed by the tall, fair haired young man who wore a simple uniform and was invariably polite and considerate.

When Josephine returned to Malmaison, the Tsar asked to call upon her. After spending an afternoon together, he was so taken with her charm and wit that he proceeded to visit her every day. Having promised Josephine that he would insure the well being of her children, the Tsar induced King Louis (who could hardly ignore the wishes of the man who put him on the throne) to look with great favor not only upon Josephine, but also upon Eugene and Hortense. At the strong "suggestion" of the Tsar, King Louis publicly congratulated Eugene on his mother's many contributions to the French people and especially "the zeal she had shown in attempting to save the life of the Duc d'Enghein."

Following the lead of the Tsar and the King, foreign dignitaries, aspiring members of King Louis' new court and much of fashionable Paris flocked to Malmaison to call upon Josephine.

Countess Walewska continued to visit with Bonaparte's son, and Josephine's old friend, Theresia Tallien came to call. Theresia was the mother of eight children by various men. Still beautiful, she had married well and was now the Princess de Caraman-Chinay.

But, no matter how gratifying it was to see the house full of guests again and to see her children safe and well regarded by the new regime, Josephine's heart was elsewhere. She confided to her doctor that, if permitted, she would have driven that instant to Bonaparte's side "never again to be parted."

She worried constantly about the state of his health and about how he was able to bear the humiliation of his fall from power. When the outspoken Germaine de Stael asked rudely if Josephine still loved Bonaparte, Josephine turned on her heel and left the room without a word. Later she confided in a friend "Do you know Madame de Stael had the effrontery to ask whether I still loved the Emperor. I, who never ceased to love him during his good fortune, how could I love him less ardently now?"

Chapter Forty-Four

The Tsar continued to delight in his days spent with Josephine at Malmaison and continued to station Cossacks on the grounds to protect her, although, now, she had little need for protection. One morning, when he came to call, he found that Josephine had a heavy cold.

"Madame, I am concerned for your health. May I have my personal doctor attend you? He is with me here in Paris."

"No, Sire, it is only a bad cold. It will go away by itself. Besides, I wouldn't want to hurt the feelings of my own physician."

"You know, Madame, I had arranged for you to have a castle in St. Petersburg; but then I thought that you would find the climate too inhospitable."

"Thank you for the thought, Sire, but I am sure you are correct. St. Petersburg would be difficult. I still miss the feel of the Caribbean sun on my skin."

"As you are unwell, I will take my leave. May I come tomorrow?"

"Of course, Sire, you are always welcome at Malmaison."

Two days later, Josephine was chilled and feverish. Yet she insisted on presiding over a formal dinner at Malmaison for the Tsar and the King of Prussia. After dinner, she danced and took a walk through the gardens on the arm of the Tsar.

In the following days, her throat became inflamed, and her chest congested. Despite a high fever, she insisted on showing visiting dignitaries the house and her art collection, and then, in the rain, showing them her garden and her zoo.

That night and in the following days her condition worsened, her fever grew higher and her breathing extremely difficult. It was soon obvious that the doctors could do nothing – that Josephine was dying.

As her children and grandchildren gathered around her bed, she lay in Eugene's arms with her eyes closed. At last, she took a long labored breath and, for a moment, opened her eyes. She whispered "Bonaparte." Then she was gone. As Eugene put it to Hortense, she went "as gently and sweetly to meet death as she had met life."

Chapter Forty-Five

The news of Josephine's death did not immediately reach Elba. When it did, Bonaparte locked himself in his room for two days, refusing to see anyone.

After that, he continued the business of reorganizing his tiny kingdom, but he did it with a heavy heart. The joy had gone from his life.

As he confided to an aide, "I should never have left Josephine. She was the radiance of my star. She was my luck; and, when she was gone from me, the touch of destiny, that seemed always to be with me, it too was gone."

Despite his depression over Josephine's death, Bonaparte remained a vital, capable – even ambitious man; and the confinement to the microscopic world of Elba gradually became intolerable. Moreover, he became obsessed with the idea that the Bourbons had been put on the throne by the Russians, Prussians and Austrians, not by the French, while, given his plebiscite, it was the French nation that gave him the throne. He began to plan a return to France, there to retake the throne. Realizing the long odds against success, he was prepared to try. After all, what more could he lose?

On the night of March 15, 1815, moving with stealth in the darkness, he boarded a small, fast boat anchored off a deserted beach on the windward side of the island. He was accompanied by a small contingent of guardsmen who had been with him on Elba. With the aid of a skilled local boatman, they were able to elude the British ships stationed off Elba to prevent Bonaparte's leaving.

At dawn, they landed at Golfe-Juan on the French Coast. Bonaparte was recognized by a few fishermen, who cheered him. Together with his contingent of guardsmen, they started up the hills leading away from the beach and toward Paris, far away.

When word of Bonaparte's landing reached Paris, there was consternation. Louis XVIII called immediately for Marshal Ney. Seated, his gouty foot resting painfully on a pillow, the king shouted.

"Ney, the monster is loose! He is making his way to Paris with a squad of guardsmen and a scarecrow group of rabble. He must be stopped before this ripple becomes a tidal wave!"

Ney smiled confidently. "Not to worry, Sire. I'll bring him back to you in an iron cage."

* * * *

Astride his black charger, Ney raised his hand, signaling his guard battalion to halt. Coming up the dusty road on foot was Bonaparte, leading a few tired guardsmen and a ragtag group of civilians, some with rifles, others with pitchforks and shovels.

"Napoleon Bonaparte," cried Ney. "You are under arrest. Have your men lay down their arms. You are my prisoner."

But Bonaparte kept walking, his guardsmen close behind, his peasant army looking less enthusiastic in the face of Ney's battalion.

"Bonaparte, I will ask you one more time. Halt! Order your men to lay down their arms!"

But Bonaparte continued to walk toward Ney, his head held high. Obviously, he was not going to obey.

"Prepare to fire," Ney ordered his guardsmen, and with a loud "clack" every rifle snapped into firing position, the front rank kneeling, those further back standing. Still, Bonaparte kept walking as if unfazed by the guns.

His squad of guardsmen, although no match for Ney's battalion, raised their own rifles. The peasant followers began edging slowly backwards.

"Take aim" came Ney's command, and the entire battalion peered, as one, down the barrels of their weapons, all aimed at Bonaparte.

Now, Bonaparte signaled for his tiny guard to stand fast, and he proceeded alone toward the menacing front of Ney's battalion. Ney raised his hand ready to give the command to fire. Then Bonaparte shouted to the soldiers whose rifles were aimed at his heart.

"Soldiers of the Guard," he cried. "If there is one among you who wishes to kill his Emperor, he can do so now."

Ney dropped his hand, shouting "fire." But there was only silence. As Bonaparte kept walking toward them, Ney's men turned to each other as if surprised that not one of them had obeyed Ney's order. Then, one at a time, they began crying out "*Vive l'Empereur! Vive l'Empereur!*" Soon, all were sounding that cry and lowering their weapons.

Bonaparte embraced as many of the front rank as he could get his arms around. Slowly, Ney dismounted and offered his sword to Bonaparte as a gesture of surrender.

"No, Marshal, this is no surrender. This is a joining of forces to march on Paris. You and I will lead."

Ney helped Bonaparte onto his own horse and, now, the battalion sent to bring him back in an iron cage formed behind him. Singing the Marseillaise, they began the long march to the capitol.

In each town along the way, the local garrison joined Bonaparte's troops, accompanied by cheering and the waiving of tri-color flags. The battalion became a regiment, the regiment a division, the division an army, and, everywhere the crowds cheered.

By the time they were 30 miles from Paris, Louis XVIII had fled – back into exile. When Bonaparte arrived at the Tuilleries, drawers were left open, beds were unmade, and lunch, uneaten, was in the kitchens ready to be served.

Carried into the Palace on the shoulders of the cheering crowd, Bonaparte went to his office, pulled a map of Europe from a cabinet and began to plan.

Later that day, Bonaparte spoke to his personal physician, sharply criticizing him for allowing Josephine to die. "Sire, it was not the disease. The Empress died of a broken heart. She told me that, had she been permitted, she would have rushed to join you wherever you were, never to leave you . . . never!"

The next day, Bonaparte went to Malmaison with Hortense. Excusing himself, he went to the room where Josephine had died. When he came downstairs, his cheeks were wet with tears.

In the following days, he set about organizing the government and starting the draft of a new constitution. But his main task was a military one – to reassemble the Grande Armee and supplement it with newly raised and trained soldiers. As anticipated, England, Russia, Austria and Prussia quickly agreed on a declaration of war.

Talleyrand, present at the assembly of these powers in Vienna, urged them on, but added the suggestion that the declaration of war be against Bonaparte personally, not against France.

"Let the French understand that we have no grievance with them. The moment they rid themselves of Bonaparte, they will have peace."

Although Bonaparte had reappointed him as Minister of Police, Fouché was convinced that Bonaparte's return would lead to disaster for France and, more importantly, for himself. He kept in constant touch with Louis XVIII, now in Holland, as well as with Talleyrand and Metternich in Vienna.

Chapter Forty-Six

By mid-June, Bonaparte was facing a combined British and Prussian force that had assembled near Brussels. The British were commanded by the Duke of Wellington, the Prussians by the aged and beloved General Blücher. Bonaparte intended to inflict a quick defeat on these enemy forces before they could be joined by the Russian and Austrian armies. He would then take Brussels, forcing Wellington and the British to leave. At that point, the Russians and Austrians would be reluctant to attack him and would sue for peace.

To accomplish this task with the necessary speed, he had to maneuver to split the British forces from the Prussians, so that he could defeat each army piecemeal. In this he was successful. By inflicting a defeat on the Prussians at Ligne, Bonaparte was able to drive them off to the North and East, moving away from the ultimate battlefield and their British allies.

Bonaparte's entire plan turned on keeping the Prussians from returning to the field before he could defeat the British. To this end, he directed Marshal Soult to convey an order to Marshal Grouchy. The order directed Grouchy to take the large French force under his command and "to follow Blücher – to be a sword in his back." Soult duly conveyed the order to Grouchy, who moved off with his force, following Blücher and his Prussians.

It appeared that the battle would be fought in a large valley between two ridges near the town of Waterloo.

On the morning of the great battle, Bonaparte stood on the Northern ridge surveying the field. Through his telescope, he could see Wellington on the opposite ridge placing his troops in defensive positions. Bonaparte knew that Wellington liked defense and would probably not attack.

By 8:00 o'clock, Bonaparte's Marshals were urging him to begin the battle. "No, not yet" he grunted. "The ground is still too muddy for our artillery pieces to be effectively moved."

"But Sire," they argued, "if Blücher returns to the field before we beat the British, we're likely finished." Bonaparte smiled. "Don't worry about Blücher. Grouchy will block him or at least delay him for a full day or more."

Finally, at 11:00 o'clock Bonaparte gave the order. A French force was to attack a British held chateau on the one side of the field and a British held farmhouse on the other. Once the chateau was taken, Bonaparte expected to envelop Wellington's right flank and roll up his entire force.

But the defenders of the two buildings were stubborn. Instead of bypassing them, the French persisted in trying to possess them, while the British held on to them in a brave and desperate defense. The battle for possession of the two sites continued for most of the day.

Meanwhile, Bonaparte sent a substantial force accompanied by cavalry to outflank the British on the other side of the field. Although they suffered severe casualties from British rifle fire, it appeared that the French would break through. But while they were in the open and vulnerable, they were hit and decimated by the charge of the British heavy cavalry under Lord Uxbridge.

The day was wearing on, and Bonaparte's army had taken severe casualties without accomplishing anything significant. Bonaparte still felt the odds were in his favor. He passed the order for a massive cavalry attack to begin.

Here Bonaparte encountered a problem of his own making. In his prior victories, his cavalry had been led by his brother-in-law, Joachim Murat, a superb cavalry officer, totally skilled in the tactics of massed and coordinated cavalry attacks. Murat had offered to serve once again, but Bonaparte had rejected him as a turncoat, which he certainly was. Bonaparte had given command of the cavalry to Marshal Ney, a brave soldier, but one lacking in Murat's experience and skill in handling cavalry.

On receiving Bonaparte's order, Ney saw the British pulling back 100 yards to better defensive positions. Assuming that they were in retreat, Ney gave the signal to his cavalry officers to start an immediate attack. At once vast lines of mounted horsemen, stretched across the entire field, began to ride across the valley toward the British guns.

Bonaparte had assumed that Ney would await the conclusion of Bonaparte's artillery bombardment of the

British positions before attacking, and, even then, would coordinate his attack with batteries of horse drawn artillery and units of infantry also at his disposal.

But Ney did neither. He simply ordered his thousands of cavalrymen to charge the British lines on the opposite ridge. Their charge was a stirring sight. The French horsemen raced across the plain, swords waiving, steel helmets and breastplates shining in the sun.

Seeing the premature charge, Bonaparte had to halt his artillery bombardment, allowing the British to maneuver so as to deal with Ney's cavalry. "What is he doing?" Bonaparte screamed to an aide. "We can't support him with our guns, and he has no infantry with him. The man is mad!"

Before Ney's cavalry reached the British lines, the British cannons fired and fired again. Row after row of French horsemen were killed. Still, they came on, in seemingly irresistible waves.

Now, a British command rang out "Prepare to receive cavalry." Instantly, the British formed into hollow squares four men deep. The front rank kneeling, the second standing, the third and fourth in reserve. The front two ranks held their bayonets before them, so that each square bristled with bayonets on all sides.

As the French cavalrymen approached the squares at a gallop, their horses shied off to the sides, refusing to charge the rows of menacing bayonets. Around and around the squares rode the frustrated French horsemen, as the British riflemen protected in the squares picked them off one at a time.

Finally, the cavalry losses were great, and it was obvious that they could not break the squares. The command was given to break off the attack and return to the French lines.

Now the British cannons that had taken shelter inside the squares were quickly wheeled out and fired round after round at the retreating French, killing many more of them.

Brave as Ney had been, his attack had been ill-planned and ineffective. Had he awaited the conclusion of the artillery bombardment and brought the French horse driven artillery with him, he could have made it difficult, if not impossible for the British to remain in their squares by firing round after round into those four deep massed formations.

Had he accompanied the cavalry attack with an infantry assault as well, he could have shattered the squares with rifle fire until they broke, allowing the cavalry to slaughter their occupants.

But Ney had done neither. His attack had been costly and in vain.

Wellington, standing in the open on the opposite hillside, turned to his aide speaking quietly, "Is this really Bonaparte facing us? The man seems just another pounder. Why would he not bring his artillery forward, fire over the heads of his cavalry preventing our forming squares until the French horsemen were upon them? Why no coordinated infantry attack? What was the man thinking?

Through his spyglass, Wellington could see the short man in the big hat and long grey coat on the opposite hill. Was this the man who had amazed the world with his military skill? Was it a double? There had been rumors of Bonaparte's use of look-alikes to frustrate would be assassins. Or, perhaps, it was just a man finally grown weary of war, less focused – even less caring.

Wellington did not know the answer. He only knew that the man in the long grey coat was not directing a first class battle – not so far anyway.

But the French were far from beaten. Fierce fighting continued over possession of the two strategically located buildings on each side of the battlefield. Except for the battle for these two key positions and some cavalry sweeps, Wellington held to his defensive positions on the hill opposite Bonaparte. As evening approached, the battle became a close-run affair in which neither side seemed able to strike a decisive blow.

Meanwhile, Grouchy's forces that had been following Blücher faced a new development. Having received a desperate message from Wellington, Blücher had turned his forces around and was returning to the battlefield. They approached Grouchy's lead elements, giving Grouchy the opportunity to assume exactly the blocking position Bonaparte had planned. His force could fight off the Prussians for hours, delaying their return to Waterloo until Bonaparte could defeat Wellington.

But the problem for Grouchy was the Emperor's order. It was most explicit. It did not say "block Blücher."

It said "Follow Blücher – be a sword in his back." The Emperor's orders were not to be taken lightly or given some unintended interpretation. Grouchy hesitated only a moment. Then he ordered his men to stand aside, allowing Blücher's Prussian force to pass unobstructed on their way to the field at Waterloo. When they had passed, Grouchy raised his arm and commanded "All right, fall in and follow Blücher! – we will be a 'sword in his back.'"

Soon Bonaparte, standing on his hill, peered with his spyglass at a cloud of dust and a group of figures moving far off in the distance. Certain this was Grouchy, he sent a courier to reaffirm that, while his men were welcome, his priority was still to prevent Blücher's returning to the field.

Within half an hour, the courier returned, leaping from his mount. "I got as close as I could, Sire. Then I received enemy fire. It's not Grouchy, Sire. It's the Prussians."

Now Bonaparte realized that Grouchy had failed and that he must overrun Wellington before Blücher arrived, or all was lost. He played his last card.

"Let the Guard advance!" he cried out. The Guard had never been beaten, had never even retreated.

As the Emperor's order was relayed, the intrepid guardsmen, each at least six feet tall and seeming more than eight feet tall in their towering beaver hats, set off in a slow, march down the hill, their drums beating a steady ominous rhythm that had repeatedly terrified their opponents throughout Europe.

As they entered the valley they could see the British

scurrying to their defensive positions and aiming their cannons. They could see Wellington, on his horse, barking out orders. They crossed the valley without breaking stride. Then, on a sudden order, they charged up the hill with bayonets fixed, still in their orderly ranks. Suddenly the hill before them exploded with cannon and rifle fire. Down went the first row. Down went the second. Still on they came, as row after row were slaughtered by the British guns.

Slowly they began to waiver, then, even more slowly, to fall back for the first time in the Guard's proud history.

They could, of course, regroup and charge again. But, suddenly, regrouping became difficult. Seeing the Guard fall back, the British charged, screaming down the hill, bagpipes blaring, guns blazing and swords waving. The Guardsmen, seeing a mass of kilt-clad madmen charging at them, prepared to fight. But, at that same moment, the first elements of the Prussian army crashed into the Guard's right flank. Waiving his sword, General Blücher bellowed orders from horseback, as the black clad Prussians began pressing the Guard inwards, crowding the French into a pocket, virtually surrounded by the still advancing British and the Prussian onslaught, which grew stronger every minute as more and more Prussians stormed onto the field.

Still the Guard held out. Orders were given to form a defensive square in the middle of the British and Prussian forces now closing in on all sides.

Suddenly, there came shouted orders for the British to halt, followed by a similar order to the Prussians. The field became strangely silent. A British officer stepped forward following a kilted soldier carrying a white flag. He shouted to the massed Guardsmen.

"Men of the Guard. You have fought bravely today. But there is no need to die. We beseech you to surrender."

With that, he ordered the British soldiers to move aside, revealing 12 British cannon aimed directly at the Guardsmen's square.

Now, a Guards officer stepped forward. "*Merde!*" he shouted, "The Guard dies. It does not surrender!"

With a quick command, the British cannons fired point blank into the massed Guardsmen, slaughtering most of them. What few were left were quickly cut down by the sabers of the British cavalry.

As it had chosen, the Guard had not surrendered. It had died.

Bonaparte, realizing now that all hope was gone, withdrew to a nearby village. He blamed no one but himself – not even Grouchy or Ney. There were tears in his eyes as he reluctantly climbed into an armored coach and left for Paris.

Chapter Forty-Seven

Bonaparte reached the capital at dawn. He seemed oblivious to the reality of his situation. He had lost still another army, and the allies would soon be in Paris. Yet he talked of going to the people, raising a force of national resistance.

His aides assured him that this was impossible, that no such force could be raised, that, as before, abdication was his only chance to save himself and, when the casualties suffered at Waterloo were known, the public would also demand his abdication. The nation was tired of war and ready to embrace the Bourbons once again as the surest way to peace.

Almost instantly, Bonaparte's belligerent tone subsided, replaced by what seemed passivity. After a futile attempt to negotiate various terms, he signed a document of abdication imposing only one condition – one on which he would not yield. His son, the King of Rome, must be made Napoleon II, Emperor of the French... even if only for a few days. The condition was finally accepted, and Napoleon II nominally "reigned" for two weeks, after which he was replaced by Louis XVIII. When Louis Bonaparte's son became Emperor in 1848, he became Napoleon III, because the King of Rome had been Napoleon II, if only for fourteen days.

Now Bonaparte began to speculate what he would do. Fouché, no longer afraid of his former master, told him that unless he left France shortly, he would personally arrest him.

Bonaparte realized that he had to leave before the allies took Paris; but, before he left, he insisted on going one last time to Malmaison. Cautioned by his aides that time was short, he would brook no interference with this plan.

When he first caught sight of the house that had played such an important role in his life with Josephine, he spoke in a hoarse voice to his aide.

"Oh, my poor Josephine! I can see her now, walking along one of the paths and picking the roses she loved so well."

Directing his aide to find accommodations in a guest house, Bonaparte entered Malmaison alone. He walked from room to room, as if in a daze, touching the things that evoked memories of Josephine – her harp, her books, her dresses, her shoes. When night fell, he wrapped himself in one of her cashmere shawls, still redolent with her scent, and slept on her bed.

Two days later he emerged to greet Hortense, whom he had asked to join him there. His aides, terrified that he would be captured, urged him to board a waiting coach at once. He refused, insisting on a few minutes with Hortense. They stood on a path lined with rose bushes. As he spoke, his eyes filled with tears.

"Your mother was the most alluring, the most glamorous creature I have ever known, a woman in the true sense of the word, volatile, spirited and with the kindest heart in the world. I know I have made some bad choices in my life, but my worst – my very worst – was parting from Josephine."

He hugged Hortense and, as they walked to his waiting coach, another coach drove into the park. Despite the frantic pleas of his aides, Bonaparte insisted on waiting to see who it was. The steps of the new coach were lowered and Countess Walewska emerged.

"I could not let you leave without seeing you again," she sobbed, running into his arms. He held her close, trying to comfort her.

"Shall I come with you – wherever you're going?" she whispered.

"No, Marie, you have the boy to think of. I will share my exile with my memories."

He moved away from her, hugged Hortense once more, boarded his coach and rode out of their lives.

By morning, he had reached Rochefort on the Atlantic coast. There, he met with his brother Joseph and a handful of loyal advisors. Where to go? Fouché had obtained a passport for him to travel to America and had arranged for him to board a blockade running frigate in the Rochefort harbor at a designated time. As Bonaparte suspected, however, Fouché had disclosed the entire plan to Wellington.

Now Joseph suggested a daring alternative. He and Bonaparte would exchange identities, and the Emperor would sail to America as Joseph Bonaparte. Suspicious of Fouché's arrangements and considering Joseph's plan generous, but unworkable, Bonaparte made his decision. He would surrender himself to the British by simply boarding a British ship in the harbor. In England, he would spend his life in a modest home in the countryside, not far from London.

He dispatched a letter to the English Prince Regent advising him that he was turning himself over to the hospitality of the British people. Then, donning his full dress uniform, accompanied by a few French officers and a number of servants, he presented himself to the captain of the British man of war Bellepheron anchored in the harbor.

The captain, who had been advised of Bonaparte's intention only an hour earlier, treated him with courtesy and had him shown to a well appointed cabin. Without delay, Bellepheron cast off and was towed from the harbor. Once past the breakwater, she raised her sails and headed for the open sea.

An hour later, a puzzled Bonaparte approached the captain on the quarterdeck.

"How soon before we reach Plymouth, Captain?"

"Plymouth? We are not making for Plymouth, sir, or any other English port. I have explicit orders to transfer you to another British vessel, which will convey you to the Island of St. Helena. The journey should take six weeks. I'm told you expected an exile in the Cotswold hills. That sir, is not to be. You will be provided comfortable quarters on a small island very far out in the Atlantic – far enough to be beyond escape."

CHAPTER FORTY-EIGHT

On St. Helena, Bonaparte worked on his memoirs, and adopted, as his frequent companion, the teenage daughter of a British officer. Bonaparte taught her games that he had learned from Josephine – blind man's bluff and pin the tail on the donkey. Laughing, they would climb the hills of the island picking wild flowers and stopping silently to look out at the sea.

Strangely, it was one of the few times in his life in which Bonaparte experienced absolute peace. The striving was over. There was nothing left to strive for.

But, as he found himself falling into the island's slow pace, Bonaparte felt his health deteriorating. This was particularly distressing, since the island's excellent Irish physician had been withdrawn on British orders. At first, it was only indigestion and headaches. But, as the months passed, the pains in his stomach became severe and his joints ached as well.

What he did not know – what the world did not know – was that the Bourbons had a different plan in mind for Bonaparte than mere exile. The British had repeatedly assured King Louis and his advisors that Bonaparte could never escape from St. Helena. But the Bourbons wished to take no chance. Only Bonaparte's death could give them the assurance they wanted. A murder would be unseemly and might arouse the enmity of the French people, who had an unfortunate tendency to forget Bonaparte's defeats and to recall only his days of glory. But a slow death from an undiagnosed illness would be perfect.

To this end, representatives of the Bourbons visited St. Helena regularly on inspection tours. Each time, they made sure that small amounts of arsenic were slipped into Bonaparte's food.

Gradually, the accumulation of arsenic in Bonaparte's body did its work. He grew weaker and the pain grew stronger. The new doctor was mystified. Finally, Bonaparte was unable to leave his bed. He was plainly dying. Soon, he lay between life and death in a semi-comatose state.

At last, he looked across the candle lit room to the officers keeping a lonely vigil. He smiled faintly and said but one word – "Josephine." Then his eyes closed.

Napoleon Bonaparte – the wonder and terror of the world – was dead.

Chapter Forty-Nine

It rained heavily at Malmaison the day Bonaparte died. It is a local legend that, at the very moment of the Emperor's death, a gardener working in Josephine's greenhouse, peered out through the pouring rain and saw a stocky male figure on the garden path. Almost immediately he saw a slender female figure glide into his arms with exquisite grace. After this, they walked together, hand in hand, up the path, until they disappeared from view.

There are those who believe this legend and those who do not. After all, the gardener only saw the pair for a moment and things seen in a driving rainstorm are sometimes misleading.

ACKNOWLEDGEMENTS

There would be no book without the skill and dedication of Bobby Woods, the efforts of Roberta Dunner, and the patience of my dear wife, Barbara.

About The Author

Bertram Fields was born in Los Angeles. A practicing lawyer, he graduated *magna cum laude* from Harvard Law School, where he was an Editor of the Harvard Law Review. After serving as a First Lieutenant in the U.S. Air Force during the Korean War, he began the general practice of law. Since then, he has tried many of the landmark cases in the entertainment, sports and communications industries and has been the subject of numerous personal profiles in magazines and newspapers. He teaches at Stanford Law School and lectures annually at Harvard.

Mr. Fields is the author, under a pseudonym, of two prior novels, *"The Sunset Bomber"* published by Simon and Schuster and *"The Lawyer's Tale"* published by Random House.

Under his own name, he has written *"Royal Blood,"* a biographical work on Richard III and *"Players,"* an analysis of the Shakespeare authorship question. Both non-fiction books were published by HarperCollins.

He lives in Malibu, California with his wife, Barbara Guggenheim, a nationally known art consultant.

MARMONT LANE
BOOKS

WWW.MARMONTLANE.COM